Bliss of Solitude

Chittaranjan Chiranjit

Translated by
Sanjeet Kumar Das

Black Eagle Books
USA address:
7464 Wisdom Lane
Dublin, OH 43016

India address:
E/312, Trident Galaxy, Kalinga Nagar,
Bhubaneswar-751003, Odisha, India

E-mail: info@blackeaglebooks.org
Website: www.blackeaglebooks.org

First International Edition Published by
Black Eagle Books, 2024

BLISS OF SOLITUDE
by **Chittaranjan Chiranjit**

Translated by **Sanjeet Kumar Das**

Cover art & Design: **Tanuj Mallick**

ISBN- 978-1-64560-568-3 (Paperback)

Printed in the United States of America

AUTHOR'S NOTE

Samuel Taylor Coleridge had once said, 'Poetry is composed of "the best words in the best order." And we can say in the similar way that short story is the best scene recreated on a small canvass. So what inspires one to write a short story? Is it just a creative pursuit or some other thing else? In my views, writing a short story or for that matter any kind of fiction is greatly influenced by two more aspects in addition to one's creative pursuit, which is inherent within the writer. These are one's ability to discern and build a narrative around the events the writer comes across, and the life of the writer itself.

The life of any person can be a story itself. But it is the author who decides which one to be picked up for a delineation of the same. Honestly speaking, I depend upon life and people for my stories and to some extent my life has also been a great source of inspiration for them.

Whether the failure of a man to purchase a piece of land or the psychological dilemma of a youth; whether the helplessness and the sense of insecurity of old parents at the fag of their life or a son becoming a monk only to give solace to his parents; whether a man's disgust towards mundane affairs after he passes through post-covid complications or one's own liking towards Gandhism or society's indulgence in vote bank politics, all these have been depicted in my stories. Similarly, the trial and tribulations, joy and sorrow, dream and despair, which are part of our everyday life and which have the potential to topsy-turvy one's life, become the contributing factors for the sketch I paint for the stories as well as for the novels. I don't know if I have done justice to each and every event and character that has found place in my stories. It is the readers and critic who will assess it in their own perspective.

So far, three short story books and six novels have been published. But, none of my stories had been translated into English Language. I feel immensely grateful to Sri Sanjeet Kumar Das, Assistant Professor, Department of English, Central University, Koraput, for his magnanimous effort to translate ten of my stories into English and publish them in a book under name 'BLISS OF SOLITITUDE'. Translation is a great work of art and requires good deal of creative talent. In that sense, Sri Das has done a wonderful job in taking my stories to a wider readers' base.

I also offer my heartfelt gratitude to Sri Tarun Kumar Sahoo, the former professor in English, an acclaimed writer and my revered teacher for taking pain in writing a preface of this volume. I also express my thankfulness to my colleagues Sukanta Kumar Seth and my friend Sanjaya Kumar Rout for their valuable suggestion and cover page designer Tanuj Mallick for making an attractive design for the book. I feel sincerely grateful to Black Eagle, an internationally acclaimed Publishing House and its owner Mr. Satya Pattnaik, Mr. Ashok kumar Parida who agreed to publish the books.

- Chittaranjan Chiranjit

TRANSLATOR'S VIEW

A young and promising writer in contemporary Odia Literature, Chittaranjan Chiranjit brilliantly knocks on the human psyche. To his credit, six novels and three collections of short stories have been published so far. This translation work, *'Bliss of Solitude',* consists of his ten best Odia short stories. These stories chosen from social, psychological, philosophical and spiritual planes are intertwined and embroidered for the general readers to go through and relish their cognitive chewing to understand human sensibility better. The profound philosophy of human life is touched upon in the work. The writer's mastery of the Odia language and thought is marked. Thoughts and feelings are artistically blended and delicately echoed together. One can understand the churned-out thoughts of the work well when the readers are in a state of solitude or a secluded place, far away from the madding crowd. I have rendered an English version of his Odia stories for the international platform to explore more and more. One can unfold the different flavours of human life in the following stories.

In the story 'Monk', a person outside renouncing his home dies. Only an old mother at home can't bear her son's death. The beloved of that person tells a lie to others that he has given up his house as a monk. However, she opened a Facebook account in his name, saying he was still alive.

Finally, when a friend of that guy reaches the spot mentioned in the account, she meets her beloved there. She also lives as a saint in the commemoration of her love.

The 'Yogi' story is based on the aftermath stage of a COVID-19 patient's critical condition and the man's spiritual consciousness in the last stage of life. The yogi's song 'bhajukinā rāmā nāmare rājan…, bhajukinā rāmā nāma…bhaji na pārile bāndhi neba kāḷa jama' is a hard and harsh philosophy of human life. Yogi's *kendara* (a stringed traditional musical instrument) spells out a mournful voice of life philosophy. Towards an individual's later part of life, the *kendara's* musical note reverberating in the ear is steadfast and determined. It may be termed 'hallucination', but it is the last truth of life. Santosh Babu is a practitioner and a representative of this truth. It is a psychological invitation to the human condition after COVID-19's critical juncture of time.

The ascetic thoughts and consciousness are enshrined in the story 'Salvation'. A widow Brahmin always lives an austere and sincere life to the Almighty. An exception is marked in her devotional lifestyle only once. Then she thinks that nobody is aware of this. Her son and daughter-in-law are always at loggerheads about this. One day, avoiding all these situational conflicts, she suddenly leaves her home to join Srikshetra, Puri.

'The Statue of Gandhi' expresses an individual's complete submission to Gandhi's thought and philosophy. If he gets rebuked by his brothers at home, he never retaliates and remains silent. His wife is worried about this. Sometimes, she questions herself how he bears all this. That man suddenly gives up his home. Searching for him, his wife comes across a person in Mahatma Gandhi's get-up. That man is her husband. She says you are getting your energy and patience to bear everything.

'Satichaura' story sheds light upon the failure and fruitlessness of a man. A piece of land is mortgaged in the village for generations. Neither his grandfather nor his father is capable of releasing that land. It is mentioned here that the young people who work in Malgodown, Cuttack, have low salaries. So he cannot release that land from the clutch of the landlord. Because of pressure from home, he told his father that he had bought a piece of land in Cuttack. After a few days, his sick father comes to a hospital in the city. Lying in the hospital bed, his father says, "Purchasing a piece of land in Cuttack is great." He then asks, "Where have you bought the land?" Suddenly, from his mouth, 'Satichaura' comes out. It is the place where people's dead bodies are set on fire for funeral rites.

In 'Sealing Wax', the philosophy and theory of human life are discussed. A professor of philosophy, giving a blindfold in his eyes, silently practices and studies his own life. But for this, he has gone to the medical and was admitted to telling a lie that he is sick. Ultimately, how he is released from the medical is about this story's essence.

'The Elephant' indirectly hints at the ''Government Rice Distribution' and 'Vote Bank Politics'. The elephant is a symbol to make human beings of their conscience and self-esteem. At last, the man runs like an elephant, and his laziness of sitting idly and the conflict of not doing anything end. The most important is one's mentality, which is brought to the limelight.

'The Last Story for My Father' is about a delusion. The

young man, a tenant, gets tied in affection with the older house owner and his wife as if they were his close relatives. They have loved him like his son. He told the house owner his name was not Chinmaya, but he called him 'Chinmaya'. The young man accepts this name. Ultimately, he discovers that Chinmaya is his son's name, who stays far away from home in the U.S.A. Here, it is a solemn narrative of a father's sorrows indirectly dealt with.

In 'The Mother's Face' story, how a sketch gets fixed in one's mind forever is penned down. For the parents, it is deeply rooted in the human psyche. Staying far away from home for several years, one tries to sketch his mother's image. The image he has made indeed resembles his mother's face, but hers is a ten-year-old image. So many things happen in the meantime. His mother's face is also changed with the advancement of age and situational needs. It's about how one's face gets changed over the years.

'The Artisan' story tells the readers how the parents make solemn vows before the deity for their children. If any mishap happens, they become worried. Here, the parents have sacrificed their lives and all their efforts for the children's betterment. Here, older parents think of their son. If they mark any deviation in the life of children, they are ready to take the onus of that misfortune and blame themselves for not fulfilling their solemn vows before the deity. As the artisans don't build the statues for them but for the public, they blame themselves and become responsible for any mistake or fault in the statue. The artisan's pain and consolation ground the essence of the story.

I have tried my best to keep the language as lucid as possible. While following the rules of equivalence and the rules of faithfulness between the Odia language and the English language, I came across some natural shifts. The culture-specific terms of the source language texts are retained as they are.

I deeply revere Chttaranjan Chiranjit for having faith in me to translate his text carefully.

I want to thank my students in the M. A. in English Programme at Central University of Odisha for their contributions to this work. They are Anjali Patra for 'The Artisan', Shanti Swarup Mishra and Preeti Ranjan Ranasingh for 'Salvation', Shibun Pattanayak and Padmalaya Thatoi for 'Sealing Wax', Udita Mishra and Lucky Sahoo for 'Satichaura' and Swati Swamprabha Bhoi 'The Elephant'. Their efforts help me take this work a step further.

I convey my heartfelt gratitude to Sri Satya Pattanaik, the director of Black Eagle Books, U.S.A. and Sri Ashok Parida of the publishing house for their kind consent to publish the texts in time.

SANJEET KUMAR DAS

FOREWORD

Journalist by profession Chittaranjan Chiranjit has carved out niche for himself in the arena of odia fiction writing. So far, he has authored to his credit six novels, three collections of short stories and a socio-political treatise tited 'Tini Dasandhira Odisha' (Odisha of Three Decades).

The book 'Bless of Solitude' is a collection of short stories culled from his three collections and translated from 'Odia into English' by Sanjeet Kumar Das. It contains ten short-stories based on a harmonious blend between reality and imagination.

'Monk' is a poignant tale of a man who was torn between spiritual and mundane desires. Lagnajit was very fond of his old friends and old memories. During Corona Virus disaster, when lockdown forced people to stay inside their houses, Lagnajit scrolled through his mobile phone to find in Facebook to his old friend Shatrujit, who had turned into a monk. His wife, Priyambada, considered it to be a futile exercise, because a monk would never be traced in Facebook.

Atlast, Lagnajit succeeded in finding Shatrujit and chats or believed to have chats with him. After the lock-down period he went to meet his friend in a house, situated at a nearly deserted place; but could meet only a nun who informed him about Shatrujit's death. In fact, Shatrujit had succumbed to an incurable disease. Shatrujit could not become an ascetic, but after his death his wife turned into a nun and led the life of a monk.

The story 'Yogi' is also about post corona virus effect. The protagonist of the story, Santosh Babu, recovered from the attack of Corona viruses but started behaving strangely. He refused to take any medicine, despite bouts of cough throughout the night. He also had a hallucination that his mother was appearing before him. Santosh Babu remembered how during childhood, while suffering from an incurable disease, he was offered to a yogi and his life was saved.

'Redemption or Salvation' is a story revolving round the conflict which an old faces with the advancement of age. Sarit's mother-in-law has lived a life of purity and austerity throughout her life. She derives a lot satisfaction from her 'pooja'-her worship of God in her 'Thakurghar' and does not feel the need of growing on pilgrimage even to Puri, the sacred place of Lord Jagannath. But, oneday Sarita discovers to her utter astonishment that mother-in-law, a life-long vegetarian, has tested non-veg food willingly. She discusses the problem with her husband, who stares at her unbelievably. However, there is a twist at the end the story. Perhaps realizing her blunder, the mother-in-law goes to Puri for her expiation of her sin.

'The Statue of Gandhi' speaks about a man who believes in peace and tranquility inside the house like Mahatma Gandhi who believed in peace and non-violence. Budhiram is the eldest among four brothers. His three younger brothers are quarrelsome and often they scolded him and try to humiliate him. Budhiram pockets the insult for the sake of peace of the house. At last, his wife does not appreciate the attitude of her husband, Budhiram.

Oneday Budhiram leaves the house and disappears. His wife searches for him everywhere, but fails to find him. On Gandhi Jayanti Day his wife meets a person dressed up like Gandhi and realizes that it is none other than her husband.

The other stories of Chittaranjan Chiranjit are also good and highly readable. Most of his stories attempt at striking a blend between spiritual quest and worldly desires. Indian tradition in general and Hindu tradition in particular permeate through his stories.

- Prof. Tarun Kumar Sahoo

CONTENT

MONK

What will you do now if you have not seen your loved ones for many years and have missed them for a long time? Having written a letter to them on a postcard, will you wait for the reply? Or, out of great anxiety, will you rush straight to them?

The desires of friendship usher in each word of the letter. In the heart's language, the letter becomes lively. The excitement of the human hearts overflows in the meeting after a long gap—stored past lurking beneath the mind spills over.

But who does all this in this age? This is the age of digitalization! In the era of Facebook, WhatsApp, Twitter, and Instagram are the latest instant communication tools! Nobody writes letters? Who maintains the friendship? Who is so much into friendship!!!

Lagnajit insists that he will write a letter to Ajatashatru first. If he does not get any reply to his letter, he will go to his village to meet him at his address.

Lagnajit's wife, Priyambada, said it's nothing but your madness. If you remember your friend, search for him with whatever social media tools you have, whether WhatsApp, Facebook, or mobile. Send message. Wait for his reply. You can ask about each other's well-being in a long chat. If you are unhappy, you can meet each other. After doing all this, you won't need anything more. Then, you won't have to meet him, said Priyambada emphatically.

Ignoring his wife's words, Lagnajit was looking for the address from the old diary. He believes that he must have written Ajatashatru's address somewhere in it. Ajatashatru was his college friend. During college, he wrote about all his happiness, sorrows, and struggles in his diary. Those were not only words but moments of fresh memories.

Lagnajit recorded facts with their permanent address, regardless of whether people would be seen and their nature would be forgotten. Everything would change, he believed, but not the site of birth. The means of communication between them will be their birth address.

Priyambada got irritated and said, you must have kept the address. I have no doubt. Have you ever thought that there will be an age of technology one day, and we will communicate through that? Why are you wasting time and sweating on that old diary without searching there?

Priyambada's words were beating against his eardrum. But Lagnajit's eyes were fixed on the pages of the diary. Lagnajit, with excitement, suddenly said, "Hey, look how I was writing about Mrutyunjaya and his address. Listen to what I have written about him. Can any mortal be in the course of life? But Mrutunjaya believes that he can. It means balancing happiness and sadness in life; he will march ahead.

That's what the victory is. Below that, you will see the address I have written.

It is your thought. Have you any news of him? Who knows if he has won life or lost the battle of life?

Priyambada asked him without showing any interest in that diary.

What do you think of me? I need to get information about Mrutyunjaya. He is what I had written about him some years ago. He answered, keeping him away from the diary.

Then, you were omniscient. Well, how could you get Mrutyunjaya after twenty to twenty-five years? Priyambada asked him with curiosity.

'...from that Facebook only. Once I was searching, I came across a friendship request from him. We contacted each other after I accepted the request. I have his phone number. Sometimes, we talk over the phone. Good and bad, joy and misery. Can't I know about him?'

You have to request a friend to be a friend. Modern tools teach that. Now you can look for him that way. If you can get Mrutyunjaya, where is the problem of calling him? Everyone is now under Facebook mania. Do you think that your friend Ajatashatru is not one of them? Priyambada asked with a little bit of anger.

He breathes heavily with an upward face. "Is it a pain of not getting an address from the diary or his inability to answer Priyambada?" he could not understand. Still, he felt that he was roaming in the clouds. Pain or futility brings emptiness. Helplessness engulfs us. We become silent in the sounds of the surroundings.

Lagnajit was silent for a while.

"It's true that you do not get his address. Now, you must try to remember whether you have written something about Lagnajit or not. That's why you are silent. Is it more difficult to search on mobile than this silence?" Priyambada asked.

Finally, Lagnajit said, looking at Priyambada helplessly. "Can I not understand what you are saying? I have got all my school friends on social media. But you can't understand why I am searching for Ajatashatru in my diary."

Now Priyambada understands that the matter is severe and submissively asked, "Why?"

He may not be on social media because he has been a monk for years.

"May he be in a secluded place, giving up everything in society; how will he be in social media?" Lagnajit was indifferent while saying.

"Monk? Since when?" Priyambada asked, understanding her mistake and Lagnajit's state of mind.

Lagnajit flinched. There is a sincere desire for a thrill in the heart to reflect on the past. It needs a stable, unwavering memory to mirror every scene from the past. It takes a pure heart full of memories to examine all of those. Lost in thought, he stopped talking.

After sometimes Lagnajit whispered, "I still remember. I have written his address with a brief note to him. I have a shady memory about it. I had written that this Ajatashatru may not be the emperor of Magadha, but he is the king of his mind and heart. He always does what he wants."

Priyambada could hear everything, though he was whispering. She asked, "If Ajatashatru has this uniqueness, he must have chosen asceticism."

Now, Lagnajit became a little restless. He could understand that Priyambada was talking like a stupid. Nobody becomes a monk/saint forcefully, he said. Anyone who is only strong-minded can travel on this saintly path.

Though he talked that way, he still felt that Priyambada was closer to the truth.

Lagnajit got up immediately. Diaries had been scattered.

Ajatashatru had been on that unwanted page somewhere in the diary.

Lagnajit was walking inside the room impatiently. "Maybe you are right, Priyam", he said. Lagnajit calls Priyambada Priyam with love.

"Has he chosen this path forcefully?" she asked.

"Not with anybody's compulsion but due to the situation," he said.

"We have not met since our college days. But after their master's, both Mrutyunjaya and Ajatashatru were preparing for competition. But in every examination, Ajatashatru failed. Then he disappeared. The failure took him that way. He became a monk." Lagnajit became anxious while talking about it.

Priyambada was shocked to see as if someone had been reborn before her. It's not a portrayal of immature youth who are tense about their jobs but of a complete life and a fully grown-up body.

Priyambada also thinks that even in complete life, there is pain and gush of disappointment.

When she looked at Lagnajit, he was looking up an old photograph of college time. Then he roared, "See, Ajata is here in this photo." But the way he stands in one corner signals that he has been forced for this photograph. He has zero interest in this. He was often absentminded like that, and we needed help understanding him correctly.

Lagnajit was asking this question to himself. Priyambada resisted and said, "I don't know if he was absentminded or you were unable to understand him, but I can't understand why you are so much into Ajatashatru today."

Lagnajit again took a deep breath. He said, "It's a horrible feeling that in this coronavirus pandemic, people leave the world daily. I am feeling sorry for that. Everyone is getting into my mind now. Who is dead now? Who has survived? This morning, Ajatashatru suddenly came into my mind. I was thinking, "Maybe he is the one who will win the race of life. We must all be dead shortly."

Priyambada wanted this topic to be stopped. So she left the spot. While departing, she said, it's fate to decide everything in life.

She returned again and said, "You know your friend is now a monk. Then why are you looking for his address? Is a Monk with any permanent address?"

For some days, I have been in this great pain—horrible feelings! I feel as if I were burned in the heat of pain in the surroundings. The place where Ajatashatru lives is the best to survive this fire. I will live peacefully and save my life if, for some days, I reside there.

Who will handle Priyambada now? She said, "I know today that you are selfish. But be aware of not stepping out in this pandemic. Go to take a bath, leaving this nuisance. What's the time now? Do you know?"

Priyambada put all the scattered diaries into the trunk. That trunk is full of memories. She also warned that she would give it to the scrap dealer if necessary. All your memories will disappear or vanish.

Priyambada has left the place. She must be busy now making breakfast in the kitchen. Ajatashatru became more critical in this conversation as if he assured in this wilderness that he was the only one safe in this challenging time. All others who are of stature are safe and lively.

After this, Lagnajit bathed, ate, and became busy. But he can't resist himself from searching for Ajatashatru.

Lagnajit did not get Ajatashatru's address from the diary. But Priyambada tried her best to engage him in different communications except Ajatashatru.

Nowadays, it has become a bad habit to get engaged on a mobile device, whether freely or leisurely, resting in the afternoon. How can Lagnajit be away from its clutch? He was also dependent on his mobile. Mobiles are one of the modern tools that have arrested everyone's mind. Mobile phones are said to allow us to travel anywhere in the world. But nobody understands that mobile phones also destroy our lives. We get worried when time flies away from us and become the mute witness of immobility. Lagnajit is arrested with that time and life, too!

Surfing on mobile, Lagnajit screamed so loud that Priambada was shocked.

Lagnajit was not only screaming but also excited. It is no exaggeration to say that just like Archimedes once shouted 'eureka'...' eureka'... The difference is that Archimedes was excited for a mathematical formula and Lagnajit for an address.

Lagnajit said in a louder voice, "Ajata.... Ajatashatru... Ajatashatru Das!!!" Is he on Facebook? How? How can it be? He asked himself many such questions and shouted again.

Priyambada came running from the other room. Seeing Priyambada, Lagnajit got a little emotional. Following your words, I randomly searched Ajatashatru on Facebook and saw him there.

"How is it possible?" Lagnajit asked, looking at Priyambada.

Priyambada smiled at Lagnajit's childish nature. How are you talking like a fool? Is there no other Ajatashatru in this world?

When I typed the name Ajatashatru, there were four to five with this name. I also thought there were many Ajatashatru. But I was shocked when I saw the profiles one by one. I at last found Ajatashatru, my friend. Look at this. This is Ajatashatru. The profile picture is of our college time. Lagnajit behaved just like a man who had achieved something suddenly.

Though Priyambada got irritated a few minutes ago, she enjoyed Lagnajit's chilling, excitement, and frenzy feelings. Do you know what I feel? Your friend has again joined this materialistic world, giving up the ascetic life?

I can't believe that, Priyam. If that's true, why has he kept only the college time photo in the profile and not his present state? Looking at Priyambada, he asked.

Priyambada had a lot on her mind. But she didn't want to prolong the matter. She just said, "Why are you worried now? You got Ajatashatru. If he is your friend, you can ask him directly now. I have said before that no man is found in any address. One can find addresses here on this mobile."

Lagnajit was absorbed in thoughts. Priyambada understood what exactly Lagnajit was thinking. Leaving Lagnajit there, she said, "Be happy to have your friend Ajatashatru. I don't have any say in it. But never think of visiting him for the peace of mind. Peace lies in the mind. It is not with anyone nor in a different environment."

Priyambada went to another room.

When Lagnajit opened Messenger on his mobile, Ajatashatru was online. It's not shocking that he is online, as he has opened a Facebook account. He got excited himself.

It is OK to send a message to someone without being friends. Now, with preparation, Lagnajit started typing. "Hello, Ajata!" Lagnajit felt as if he would be offline after receiving this. He kept thinking, 'Is it a fake I.D.?' Then he said to himself, no, it's not. If it were, what would one say about this college photo? At that time, neither the camera nor the mobile was there. A few of us rarely took pictures, or the cameraman would come and shoot in the college.

Lagnajit stopped for a while in this thought. When he looked at his phone, he got answers from Ajatashatru and a few questions from him… eager to know many things.

Fondness to search for something and fortune to get that bewilders a person. The condition of Lagnajit was like that.

Both of them chat for a long time. It's not a conversation; it's a reminiscence of the past. Past became present when memory was memorized. Present mixes in the past as if the past was never the past. This present is not of this time, not even of this moment.

Lagnajit felt that Ajatashatru was more excited to know about him. It's natural. Ajatashatru is a saint; what's about him? Of course, he could ask, but what will he ask? Strict rules restrain the life of a saint. There are no challenges but the attraction of systematic life. He lives in the ashram, a unique, calm world. Lagnajit and Ajatashatru were going back to the past rather than the present. Ajatshatru asked many things as if he had forgotten all the college moments. Forgetting is natural. But Lagnajit kept on remembering all things.

In the end, Lagnajit asked a few questions.

Well, say, are you a monk now? And if yes, why are you still having the name?

For a moment, Ajatashatru became silent. He replied that he would answer every question in the meeting.

Lagnajit said, in the meeting? Yes, I wanted to meet you. And do I have to wait for some days? Just tell me, where are you? Due to this shutdown period, it's impossible to reach you; I will be there after this. Let me know your phone number. I will be happy and relaxed to talk to you sometimes. Or else, where will I get mental peace in this present time?

You don't have to go anywhere else, Ajatashatru replied. Or I don't have to give you my number. Do you know 'why'? I am now living in your city.

Giving the address of a nearby place, Ajatashatru went offline.

Such a friend you are; what is the language of saints? Lagnajit was in so many questions that he seemed like a sculpture from ancient times. Sometimes, man becomes a stone while living in this world.

Lagnajit is unaware that Priyambada is behind him and has asked for something. He looked once at Priyambada as if he were struggling with an invisible thought. Then, in a soft voice, he said, you will be surprised to know that Ajatashatru is in this city, but I have not known.

.It would help if you were happy that Ajatashatru is in this town. Why are you upset like this? Priyambada asked indifferently.

'I am unhappy because I can't reach him immediately due to this shutdown. I have to wait a few days, though he is near me,' said Lagnajit.

I will ask if you are OK with it. Getting an approving nod from him, Priyanka said, "Ajatashatru, whom do you want to meet? Why is he here in this city? Is he a monk or just making all fools and puzzles? Or, many years before, he has been distracted. Or has he returned from halfway?

With some irritation, Lagnajit said you insult the saint more than my friend. You will see he would be changed after meeting me once.

The shutdown lasted for several days. Released from this coronavirus situation is the only way. But only a few days later, Lagnajit did not yet think of Ajatashatru. After that day, due to an offline connection, I can't be there. Instead, enthusiasm increased. Another fear was that he would return to his ashram after the shutdown.

Saints are always absorbed in one 'Being'. They are here now, and they won't be here at the same time. The same is the case of Ajatashatru.

As soon as the shutdown ended, Lagnajit became more anxious. The attraction of meeting a childhood friend and an irresistible desire to get rid of depression led him to that place—that address that Ajatashatru gave.

Ajatashatru said a big Banayan tree is there, and at a little distance, there is a single house. He lives there.

Lagnajit reached and saw there was a house. It is the house of a middle-class individual. Why is Ajatashatru here? He thought it was a temple or monastery. He must be living there! But why is he here? That house is locked. But he was shocked when he saw the nameplate as it carried Ajatashatru Das. Is Ajatashatru das a permanent resident here? Is this the truth that he has been hiding for many years, and there is nothing like a monk? Lagnajit thought.

Even though the gate was closed, Lagnajit could not return from there as if he were examining himself beneath that tree, as if it was asking, 'You are serious or me?' In silence and seriousness, there was hope in the heart of Lagnajit that Ajatashatru would return.

After sometimes someone returned. It was not Ajatashatru but a middle-aged woman. Her dress code is like a nun's. She unlocked it and got in.

Nameplate of Ajatashatru, a nun!! Lagnajit couldn't understand anything, as if trapped in a maze. He felt 'Ajatashatru was a bundle of complicated puzzles.'

He heard 'you must be Lagnajit' when thinking about this. Lagnajit was startled. When he turned, that lady was standing near him.

A shaky reply came from Lagnajit's mouth, 'I am Lagnajit. But who are you?'

You will know me later, but that woman said I was the one who called you here.

Are you the one who has called me? Then I felt deceived when you opened my friend's fake I.D. Lagnajit growled.

I have not lied. But when I knew you were his friend, I thought I would call you and tell you something hidden for a long time. With the hope that one day I would find someone like you, I opened this Facebook account. That woman said so, staying in the dock.

"His stored memories? Is the Facebook account in Ajatashatru's name? Oh, what are you talking about?" Lagnajit asked all these at a time, and he stood up silently for answers as if his eyelids were shrinking from the vast ocean to a point.

But that woman's eyes stretched to the vast horizon; emptiness buzzed in comprehension. She said with a moist voice that he accepted me as his wife before he left the world forever. You may call me his wife or fiancée; he was the only man of my heart, the man I loved.

Well, why did he become a monk again? Lagnajit asked.

'Monk? He was not a spiritual pilgrim but rather a traveller of death.' cried the woman.

'The mortal world? What are you saying?' Lagnajit screamed.

Yes, of the mortal world!!! While he died of an unknown disease, keeping his head on my lap, he said at his home, his old mother lives. She can put up with the fact that he is a monk but can't bear the pain of his death. That woman cried saying this.

Now it's all clear in front of Lagnajit. He saw that woman very closely. She had lit as if she were a light with a pure heart.

He couldn't ask more about Ajatashatru, nor could he stay there. Lagnajit just asked her while returning, "Why are you here? And in this attire?"

After deciding to be alone for the rest of my life, the last word that came out of his mouth was probably his desire. And it leads me to live a life like that. How have I reached here like this while roaming here and there? Unable to cope, the woman entered the house, leaving Lagnajit alone on the road.

Inside the house, Lagnajit heard a strange sound intermittently. For him, whether it is a mournful song or an invited call in obsession.

By that time, there was broad daylight all over the surroundings. In that scorching ray, two people were burning. One is his friend Ajatashatru, and the other one is this woman. And the third one is Ajatashatru's mother. In some far sky, she must have been one of the stars. Has she been crying while alive, or shedding tears at the loss of her son or offering flowers? There, Priyambada, as she will be eagerly waiting for him or in an agitated state?

That day, Lagnajit saw the photo of Ajatashatru's last ritual. There are a lot of tributes in the comment box. Many questions were there with homage.

Lagnajit also wrote:

Farewell monk!!

All spirits are also monks!!!

YOGI

Not to win, Mr. Santosh wanted to stick to his stubbornness. He recently retired from the job and was bereft of any work for the time being. If employment and retirement are two stages of life, he has already stepped onto the second stage. But he is not ready to accept it. He says, "Now he is a pilgrim of a new stage of life. Here lies the real test of life.

He led a systematic, calculative, and disciplined lifestyle during his service period. Now, the life he will experience will have no pressure, restraints, or routine processes, or he must live within its limitations. While living in this phase, it's only the age that advances. The rest will reach him in a moment or a day. In due course, he will also lose them.

Everyone seemed surprised by Santosh Babu's insistence. He is adamant that he will never retake medicines. Going to the Doctor or taking medication is not the only option for curing him.

The entire family was stunned as they listened to Mr Santosh's words. He returned home after spending a few days in the hospital for COVID positive. He insists that he was cured but not by medicines. After hearing this, the entire family became tense. He is now fifty-nine. When one...two...three years pass one after the other, the body rapidly deteriorates. Does its effect continue? Physical ailment! If you are physically ill, the only way to get over it is to take medicine. So, how can he make such a choice? It's difficult to say how dangerous it will be for him if he sticks to his decision. Perhaps he was unable to guess. That's why he is saying this.

Sumati, Mr Santosh's wife, observed her son-in-law's preoccupation and stated, "Father was in the COVID hospital for a few days due to Corona." He was on a ventilator and given oxygen due to his critical health condition. That might to have caused him a lot of grief. He is disheartened after being away from his family for a few days. That is why he is delirious. It's all about the health issues! Nobody knows anything can happen at any time. He will take medicine if he gets sick.

Partha became silent after realizing the truth of his mother's words. He was also convinced that his father expressed all this out of emotion. There is a wide gap between what we say and practise in the real world.

Partha, on the other hand, was baffled. Why is his Dad taking such drastic steps after returning from the COVID hospital? What circumstances compelled him to do so? Partha's wife (Santosh Babu's daughter-in-law) Bidisha said, "If anybody was hospitalized for Corona, how important was the oxygen cylinder for the patient than the medicine?" What is the need for this medicine when oxygen is naturally available to us and essential for the good health of every human being? Perhaps Dad has taken this step for this reason.

Partha was unable to accept or reject Bidisha's words. But no one can question his father or discover why he has in determined to do so.

Sumati was looking forward to the day when he would require the medication to feel satisfied. She did not want his body to weaken. She has prayed immensely to God for Santosh Babu's recovery from illness. When he was admitted to the COVID hospital, she spent hours sitting in the *Thakur ghar* (a room specially designed for worshipping God in one's house), and only she knew how many tears she had said. He thinks he will take medicines in case of emergency. In a situation, a person is compelled to make a decision. That particular decision gets modified in another. Sumati stated differently that no decision is permanent. Her faith disintegrates at Santosh Babu's insistence, just as the window's glass panes dismantle when stones are pelted at repeatedly and break into pieces.

The story of the last night! When everyone was asleep, Santosh Babu suddenly started to cough. Sumati thought something had stuck in his throat. But despite his continuous efforts, he could not get rid of the cough in his stomach. Instead, the cough he was trying to suppress within his body had come out with a loud noise and spread out not only in his house but also outside their house. Everyone awoke in Santosh Babu's paroxysmal (whooping) cough. Along with his wife and daughter-in-law inside his home, the neighbours surrounding their building were disturbed.

Santosh Babu was trembling from the cough. His veins and arteries seemed to be bursting. Sumati was worried. She stood up with a cough syrup. It's not time to test whether Santosh Babu accepts it or not. Instead, she aims to relieve him from the cough's pain.

Then darkness might be outside, but a grey light was scattered inside. In that light's diminishing impact,

Santosh Babu's face was twisted with pain. He was sitting on the bed, but his entire body appeared to have rested on his hands. Sumati could decipher the expression of the face dangling in that shade of grey light. She could not bear him to suffer.

At last, she continued, "Take a sip from this syrup." It will quit coughing. You won't be able to have a sound sleep tonight, otherwise. No matter how much she tried, Santosh Babu didn't pay any heed to her words.

After listening to Sumati's words, he looked up and stayed in that position. Sumati understood what he wanted to say. As a result, she didn't request him to have the syrup again. She sat on the bed, entirely religiously, lest her husband should understand her suffering. Then, he will rest after taking medicine. The husband's pain, like the coronavirus, infects her!! That infection and injury is like a stage of earning pride for her.

The whole night, he was suffering or whooping from that cough. He alone is aware of his level of pain. But Sumati was also burning in that pain. Additionally, the son and daughter-in-law became worried with each blow of the cough.

Towards morning, he slept for a while. Sumati was raising the bed carefully so his sleep would not be disturbed. He thought his decision was as firm as the mountain. Otherwise, how could he not have taken the syrup after suffering a lot?

When he woke up, the cough had subsided. This was not magic. Santosh Babu knows that once started, the cough will not go away so quickly. Many times, a light cough rises to reach the mouth. He suppresses the cough.

So, how long can he hold it in his mouth? While thinking about this, his son's phone rang, and Partha was probably phoning the DoctorDoctorDoctor. He would be content if he were unaware of the Doctor'sDoctor'sDoctor's words. Still, Partha echoed the Doctor'sDoctor'sDoctor's remarks. "Would he like to tell him or repeat the situation?" he assumed. "Cough can persist even after recovering from COVID," we should not worry. Partha was silent after that. The Doctor must have prescribed medication. His helplessness is this silence.

Sumati appeared holding a glass filled with a saffron-coloured liquid while Santosh Babu was absorbed in thoughts and said, "This is the boiled water mixed with ginger and bay leaves." Sip this; the cough will undoubtedly vanish. Santosh Babu accepted his wife's 'homemade remedy' without hesitation. He was aware that doing this would help stifle the cough for a while to some extent. So, is this cough the only thing causing him pain? He asked himself this question and blinked. Is he infected with whooping cough or another serious illness?

There is a sound of coughing so that the family can hear. Many diseases do not have sounds; those deteriorate a person internally. Others need to understand only the pains. After thinking about this, Santosh Babu's chest felt heavy again. This chest pain started last night. While coughing loudly, the chest suddenly felt tightened. He was tagged with unbearable pain. At times, he was breathless. He had a mild fever. And when he coughed, his chest was shaking. Though he coughs a bit, the chest pain is still afresh inside.

But Santosh Babu must bear this. He knows well that

the family members are not forcing him to take medicine because he does not pay so much attention to coughing. When they hear about chest pain, they will take him to the hospital and starting from E.C.G. to haemoglobin, all the tests will be done. And, once you fall into the medical trap, where will you go if you don't take medicine? What he has promised, he does not want.

As Santosh Babu was contemplating this, he trembled in pain equally. The more he tried to stop it, the worse the pain he felt inside. That he was surviving the pain, Sumati returned inside the house as he attempted to squeeze his chest to relieve the pain.

"Are you observing how the entire body perspires and is messy now?" Let me use a cloth dipped in warm water over your body for quick relief. It will comfort you. "No. Thanks; I don't know why I am with a mild temperature now," he said, trying to hide all his physical pain and act normally.

Sumati was afraid of hearing that his body was 'warm'. Is it not a fever? Sumati enquired. 'No, it didn't happen,' he said, relieving Sumati of her concerns. Yes, I coughed throughout the night, so I felt a little warm inside. The pain in his chest suddenly doubled with the cough. He wanted to roll around on the bed while holding his hands to his chest. Alternatively, he was unable to accomplish it at all. He is, therefore, a defenceless man whining.

Who has ever seen their entire pain mirrored on their face? However, Sumati was able to read out Santosh Babu's pain. But unable to take any further action, she asked, "Can you bear such pain?" or won't you take any medicine? I don't know why you're insisting on this. You don't tell me when I ask. Now, you must have understood the repercussions of your insistence.

Santosh Babu's cough was also heaving. The whole day, he struggled with that cough and became unconvinced. That's the time the pain was worsening. That was unbearable! He endured the agony and retained the sound "Oh!" He knows that even a slight increase in this word could further shatter the family members. How long will he live if his family is devastated?

He asked this time, not to anybody but to himself. 'Santosh Babu! Can you say why you are with this obstinacy?' While this question turned up in my mind, someone hung a curtain before the horizon. As the paintings are over, now the curtain is drawn. Now, let's face the reality.

Why are you with this obstinacy?

Is it stubbornness or satisfaction?

Abruptly, the enduring image of his stay at the COVID hospital appeared before his eyes. As soon as the ventilator kicked in, he believed that his natural life had ended. The rest of his life will only be artificial. This artificial life can end at any point in time. He appears to be a parting traveller at this point.

Suddenly, his mother's face began to move around while tears were streaming from the corners of his eyes.

My mother's face after so long! That, too, is at this juncture of time. The nephew in the village calls and reminds him not to eat non-veg items on her 'Death Anniversary'. That is again at his elder brother's warning. When he remembers, he asks himself, did he recognize his mother's 'death anniversary'? If he remembers the day, how long will it take to forget? In preparing the death anniversary food, the mother comes to his mind, and it seems forgotten after that.

But why is my mother remembered now? Why did she appear in this last stage of my life? As she was recalled, he remembered the trivial incidents of his childhood. He remembered how a tender voice shone from Santosh Babu's heart and his urge to cry and roar the surroundings.

She said to him, waving her hand, "You have suffered a lot. Now, it's time for you to leave the world."

How will he leave?

His childhood memories floated before him: The Yogi was singing with a stringed musical instrument in the village courtyard, *"bhaju kinā rāma nāmare rājana...bhaju kinā rāma nāma...bhaji na pārile kulachandramāre... bāndhineba kālajama re kumara ..... bāndhineba kālajama..."* His mother had taken him in her hands and followed the ascetic from door to door.

Once in his childhood, he had a fever and was ill for fifteen days. Though he was under severe medication, there was no improvement in his health. After two of her sons passed away in their early stages of life, this sick baby was in her arms. The grandmother told my mother that she should surrender this baby to a Yogi. Yamaraj will never touch him again. She found Yogi beside him and said, 'I am leaving my son in your custody. Bless him for the speedy recovery of his health.' He was not sure about the authenticity of her statement, but he gradually recovered from his illness.

When he grows up and becomes ten, he should be released from the Yogi after donating the Yogi a bowl of rice, some cash, some vegetables, and a rosary. He should have dressed himself in Yogi's attire to beg with a bowl requesting alms from ten villagers. After that, he ought to be freed with Yogi's blessings to go to their home.

But people needed clarification about the Yogi's whereabouts. "Why do you think of that, Yogi?" said my grandmother at the maternal uncle's house. Instead of that Yogi, any Yogi can be invited and released after the rituals. "He is someone's son, and someone else will free him?" the villagers opined. My father got irritated and said, "Is it necessary to release him from the Yogi?" My mother said, "You won't believe all this ". But he is called 'Yogi' throughout the village. Can you deny them all? My father got annoyed and said, 'Let the name Yogi be removed from this day.'

Santosh Babu could recall everything. That time, his mother's eyes were filled with tears.

Where is his mother now? Where is Yogi? Where is the name Yogi?

Santosh Babu's eyes were full of tears. He thought how significant this hospital, this medicine, and this pain were in front of her mother's face.

Santosh Babu returned home and was cured from the hospital. He believed the mother was hovering around him in an angelic (non-physical) form. That is why she has come to take him away from the Yogi's hands. She has tried many times in her life. In the past, when she had heard that his health condition was not good, she cursed herself. Her futility in releasing him from the Yogi overwhelms her every moment. Then, she even said, 'That is the reason behind his lousy body.'

"How is it possible?" Santosh Babu asks her mom. "Were I still the son of the Yogi, an invisible power would protect me from any danger. I should not be inflicted with any disease. Why am I fallen sick sometimes?"

She smiles a bit. Her regret drops down in her dry smile. Whether she is near or far, Santosh Babu can measure her sorrow. She says, 'You are only for name sake, Yogi. You neither remained like a yogi nor obeyed the rules. Your name is also not 'Yogi'. You are suffering the consequences of that, my son!'

Santosh Babu understood well what his mother was hinting at his father. He was asking again, 'Where did that Yogi go? Now, how will I get rid of that? Will I be like this for the rest of my life?

She cries and says, 'He is the only hope. He has helped you rise from deathbed and given you a new life.' He says, 'All this is just one of your beliefs. Nowadays, some medicines and types of equipment have been invented to cure diseases. You will see how my body recovers from illness, and I will get better whenever I am ill". While crying, my mother says, you are also talking like your father.

The treating Doctor knows how he recovered from COVID-19. But, Santosh Babu realizes that his mother's touch is behind her recovery. Today, again, his mother comes to him in every pain and every breath. Her face rose and danced in front of him. Partha entered the house while he was looking closely at his mother's face. After that, Sumati and Bidisha joined.

Parth was saying, 'Lo, you see the time now. Dad has not got up? There must be some health issues. Or he needs to tell us the facts.

Sumati, Santosh Babu's wife, became conscious. Maybe, scared by the fear, she went to Santosh Babu and caressed him. But Santosh Babu had returned to his pre-childhood state with this inexplicable touch once more. How could it be as tender as his mother's touch?

"It won't work if we will listen to Dad anymore," declared Partha. I am calling the Doctor immediately. Sumati and Bidisha also backed Partha's decision.

Santoshbabu was warned, knowing that the Doctor was coming. However, he could not protest. He knew that his voice would be lost to the voices of three people. Can the voice of a sick person be heard?

Waiting for a doctor is not a fleeting movement but a stored and transmitted belief. Santosh Babu was happy again when everyone left the place with that hope. With him were only his mother's face and the chest pain. It was evening. Sumati then proceeded to the *puja* room (for prayer). The daughter-in-law, Bidisha, went to her room. Before the Almighty, Sumati will lament requesting for her husband's recovery. It has already been four months since the birth of her grandson. Bidisha will be very busy for him. Partha must have consulted the physician as well. This is how the life's journey runs.

There was a pin-drop silence in the house. Suddenly, a musical voice reached his ear:

"*bhaju kinā rāma nāmare rājana...bhaju kinā rāma nāma...bhaji na pārile kulachandramāre... bāndhineba kālajama re kumara ..... bāndhineba kālajama...*" That voice...that tune.

He couldn't sleep anymore. Pushing back all the pain, he woke up in a rush, full of excitement. The family might say this is an excuse for him to ignore the Doctor. Then, it seemed to him that voice was ringing here. And this voice alone can relieve his pain. He put on a shirt. At first, he thought he couldn't go out. With his sick health, can he move and take out a step?

He fortified his mental strength. He felt as though his chest was not the source of his agony but rather his thoughts. He decided what he was going to do and stepped forward. In the colony where he lives, there is a dreary deserted road. Before that, would he cross some buildings next to his house? But he thought that the music was coming from somewhere nearby. He was dragging his weak foot forward. He seemed to feel that someone was helping him walk on the road. He was not walking himself.

Silence pervades everywhere. By that time, he walked far away from home. The deep voice that he had been so drawn to suddenly became louder. Santosh Babu thought the voice was coming from a nearby place. The tuning of the *kendara* (a traditional musical string) is floating around. When he stood up with a steady heart, he realized the voice came from a house a little away from the roadside settlement. It was not only the musical beats but also the song partially heard.

He couldn't move ahead from there. Anyhow, he managed to walk up to that house; he sat on the porch and couldn't enter the house. Suddenly, an elderly man came out of the house and asked, "Who are you looking for, son?" At first, Santosh Babu looked at that older man religiously. Then he said, 'Someone was playing the *Kendra*, uncle. I came to listen to him.'

"Do you enjoy listening to hymns, son? I was the one

to play the instrument. Do you want to hear? Wait, I'm singing along with music."

The older man went inside. The same "*bhaju kinā rāma nāmare rājana...bhaju kinā rāma nāma...bhaji na pārile kulachandramāre... bāndhineba kālajama re kumara ..... bāndhineba kālajama..."* voice. He was getting excited hearing that song. It would be a fantastic pain reliever if it weren't a song.

Santosh Babu was engrossed in that song and looking for his mother and Yogi. The old man approached him and asked, "Who were you looking for, son?" What were you looking for? You are always with me and in my soul.'

He was surprised. 'Am I with you?' he inquired. How is it? I am still in my family members, Yogi. I travelled such a distance only to hear your music.

The older man smiled a little. He said brokenly, 'If I had not been with you with my song and music played on *kendara* instrument, why would you have come here? That is why I know that though you're far from me physically, your mind, knowledge, and consciousness always rest with me in my domain.

Then the old man added, pausing, 'I know you're suffering for this.' I won't keep you in trouble anymore. I am releasing you from my bonds as of today. Now, you can go.'

Someone nearby appeared to laugh at this point. Is it my mother? A feeble voice came out of Santosh Babu's heart.

He has no idea how long he has been in his unconscious state, but somehow, he gets up at Partha's command. Partha said Doctor Doctor has been waiting for you for a long time. How come you are here? How did you travel such a long distance? And your body is weak. How long have we been searching for you?

'I stopped here for a while to listen to the old man's *Kendara* instrument,' Santosh Babu explained. His father's words stunned Partha. What exactly are you talking about, Dad? Is this a shattered house? No one is here?'

Santosh Babu was stunned. 'No one is here? So, who is he?' 'Who was singing the song that I listened to a long time?'

He had no idea when he returned home with his son. It appeared to him that his mother, not his son, was holding his hand and leading him. The rage within him shatters his rage and ego, bringing him back to reality and restoring the intoxication of life.

After arriving at the house, his mother, who is in an invisible form, drops his hand and diminishes with darkness, nature, earth, and creation. 'Suddenly, the unuttered word *Maa.... ....!*' came out of Santosh Babu's mouth.

Sumati came out of the house. She took his hand and led him inside, saying, 'Why do you always talk like this when you're not feeling well? Mother's spirit must be in trouble like you. Besides, the kids have also grown up. Why are you behaving like kids? What would they think?

There was no doctor in the house. The DoctorDoctorDoctor waited for him and then walked away, irritated. 'Dad is an example of what experts say is that patients lose mental stability after the release from COVID-19,' Partha said to Sumati and Bidisha, who were in a state of confusion. The refusal to take medicine stems from within him. Instead, you say for so long, Dad had experienced not physical but mental anguish.

Santosh Babu smiled slightly for a while. The family was reassured by his smile. He was more self-assured than that. Along with that, his audacity transformed into a distinct emotion or feeling. The pain had vanished. But was that physical or mental?

SALVATION

The sun shines brightly from mid-April to mid-May in the village courtyard. The sun's searing heat doesn't deter a *Kirtana Mandali* (a group of traditional musicians and singers usually lost in devotional singing)—the members of the group strike about the rhythmic movement of their feet with their unique postures. The drums, tabors and cymbals are resonating throughout the space.

Crash! Clang!...Crash! Clang!

All members in the troupe chant the name of Hari (God Vishnu) and the name of the holy land of Vrindavan in their devotional singings and offerings.

'The flute's sweet and resonant sound is heard. Is Vrindavan nearby?

'Oh, Brother! Hey Brother!! How far is Vrindavan from here?'

What's in this *Harinam*? The entire village seems to chant the name of that celestial abode, Vrindavan. Every nook and corner of the village is surcharged with this religious thought and vigour.

With her heart and soul, Sarita can't enjoy seeing or hearing anything there. Her mind is torn apart between falsehood and truth. It's a big enigma. Who's lying? Who's telling the truth? It takes a lot of work to decide between the truth and falsehood. That is where the conflict centres around.

All this sea of questions is as unsettling as the waves roar to disturb her mind incessantly like a baby calf racing and stirring her belly.

She can't decide where to settle: the vast ocean courtyard or the calf's steady portrait of racing!!

She thinks that falsehood and truth are contrastive concepts that stand diagonally opposite, like sunrise and sunset. We can follow the directions if we need to follow them correctly. Certain things must be gauzed; otherwise, we can't verify whether they are true or false. A lie may be true, and the truth may appear untrue. Sarita often confronts that situation.

Before her eyes lie the face-off between truth and falsehood-her mother-in-law and her only son, Chiku, the two characters standing side by side.

Chiku says...

'I have seen...looking at the surroundings, you entered the house like a cat. Bringing a bit of the curry soup from the pot, you put it on your palm and sipped it into your mouth.'

Having heard this, her mother-in-law ventilates anger. Her entire body shakes and spits filthy language.

"O scoundrel! How dare you accuse me of false allegations? Dharma won't forgive you.

Sarita gets startled. Does mother-in-law scold? Again, to Chiku, the only grandson?

Chiku is single-winged. Whatever comes to his head, he will start swaying. He won't listen to anyone; nothing can control him, even his mother-in-law's scolding.

Nagarkirtan (a processional singing of holy hymns by a group in the residential areas) returned to the place a few hours ago. Along with the rhythmical chanting of *Asthaprahari* (a Hindu ritual function performed in praise of Lord Krishna), Manu Das will revolve around *Chaura* (the raised platform with a *Tulsi* plant) outside the home seven times while carrying an earthen pot filled in curd and other ceremonial items. When youngsters apply dust and sand mixed with water to their bodies, elderly persons smear this like sandal paste on their foreheads for their recovery from illness and suffering.

Liberation is inevitable. Sarita pondered over. If Chiku is right, family tradition will collapse. The entire family will be sinful if they don't get rid of it. We will be stirred inside. Is it a trifle? It is one of the great sins mentioned in the scriptures of the entire human race.

Her mother-in-law is sad and perplexed. She was struggling with *Purusartha* in her last stage of life. That is marked on her face.

What can Sarita do?

Mother-in-law is on one side, while on the other is her blood. She is quiet and worried because of this. Otherwise, she could have controlled Chikku by this time. She does not dare to say anything or challenge her mother-in-law today! She decided not to respond to that. It's better to maintain silence. Silence is also dangerous. Though not contrary to belief, it is a spider web of countless questions.

By that time, the quarrel between mother-in-law and Chiku has stopped. Chiku was ready to move outside. Sarita's gesture to him was that he would not spread this outside.

With a heavy face, her mother-in-law entered the other room.

Sarita knows Chiku's mockery and her mother-in-law's rage are like the bubbles in the water. That no one in the neighbourhood had heard about this also relieved Sarita. Otherwise, it would have been very critical. The family would have been embarrassed if the neighbours had insisted or hammered on it.

Sarita again thought – The weakness inside the mind and the simplicity outside will never assure brilliance to any person. In the same vogue, it is unsurprising that the mind will be peaceful, even if the outside world is chaotic.

When she thought this, Sharita looked at her mother-in-law again.

The skin has got wrinkled. The power of her virtue has adhered to her body. That's why, after having wrinkled skin, she is glowing. But who knows that her heart is a little impure or unholy? She believed Chiku one hundred per cent that someone would stress it. When she thought about why she felt this, Sarita had already reached the front door.

The village courtyard lies beneath the main door of the house—a row of houses ahead. The village is the storehouse of many mysteries and oddities. Glory means the root of social bonds (societal relationships). Hamlets have been formed based on caste for ages. These are *Brahmin Sahi, Karan Sahi, Gowda Sahi, Daroit Sahi, and Harijan Sahi...* nobody can see any difference in celebrating *Mela Mahotshav* and festivals in different hamlets of the village. Ironically, despite the immeasurable changes of time, some old-fashioned ideas and their customary practices-cum-rituals are still strong in people's minds.

That also surrounds the *Brahmin hamlet* adjacent to the temple. Twenty to twenty-five houses are in that hamlet. The geographical condition of the hamlet has changed, and in due course of time, changes have also been perceived. If an untouchable walks in the village courtyard, there is no need to sprinkle cow dung-mixed water, or if the smell of wine or meat in hamlets spreads outside, nobody vomits.

However, the Brahmin society remains strict and particular about treating widows of noble descent.

Widows may or may not wear the rosary of *tulsi* plants on their necks, but they won't wear jewellery on their necks, ears, or hands. They will never wear colourful *saris*, maybe lower or higher prices! It's an unpardonable sin to talk of meat or chicken; even to look at them is strictly prohibited! Visiting Jagannatha Temple, Puri in other months, except Kartik, observing *Habisha Vrat* (a religious observance held in the month of Kartika in which the devotees take a single meal a day consisting of boiled rice and clarified butter) for blessings of the Almighty is forbidden!

Sarita closed the door and went inside. The curry pot was boiling. Sometimes, the spicy dissolved comes out of the vessel's cover. Sarita removed the cover. The entire house was filled with vapour. The steam hints at how delicious curry her cooked food is. Sometimes, a man is judged by his self-restraint power. Because it is esurient that makes a person indecisive, Sarita thinks that her mother-in-law will forget the rituals and social customs of her temptation to taste the food.

One does not lose self-control in the old age. During one's lifetime, the *Akhandadipa* (unbroken light of a lamp), which burns in the mind for self-purification, does not allow it to be extinguished. Sarita was worried as she thought her mother-in-law would be an exception and adopt a changed/new lifestyle.

She also thought...

There will be the need for cleansing as per rules if the mother-in-law realizes and confesses it as a sin. If not, there will be sin for three generations. Since time immemorial, are punishments prescribed in religious scriptures for this offence? She has to stay in the eaves of the house. She has to follow the rules and regulations strictly. But our predecessors conversing in the scriptures outlined the paths for emancipation. There is no other way to overcome this sin. After offering *pinda* (balls of rice) to the River Ganga and the River Gaya, she has to offer '*Badapinda*', the '*Safli Shraddha*' at home.

Sarita returned to the front room or drawing room. Mother-in-law was sleeping in her house. It was understood from her sleep that some internal conflicts had troubled her entire body. Her hands over her forehead indicate how much concerned she is.

She has known her mother-in-law for some years. Mother-in-law never sleeps like this. She helps others understand the traditional duties of the family well. She says executing the traditional practices well is the best religion. She has just got up from bed. She said to me that she was not we. Who knows? The attached door would be permanently closed if a net curtain hung in the mind's room. Nobody can see anything inside.

From the beginning, Sarita marked her mother-in-law and thought about her deeply. She has recently come to an in-law's house as a new daughter-in-law. After reading the Bhagavat, her mother-in-law called. Sarita is very much afraid. She has yet to understand her mother-in-law well to date. Sarita reached the *puja ghar* made for worshipping God. The door was half-closed. She went to the door and stood there. Mother-in-law called her inside. The mother-in-law was sitting before God as if shining in the holy land. Every house will be a paradise if there is temperance, diligence, sanctity, and religious spirit.

The eyes of the mother-in-law are half-closed like a meditative monk. Sarita quietly sat next to her mother-in-law.

Mother-in-law said-

"Try to understand, my daughter'... Surrendering yourself entirely before God is the best and most straightforward approach to soothe your soul and your family from the high ordeals of this chaotic world. I will be glad and pleased if you engage yourself in worshipping and reading religious scriptures earnestly daily. Sarita can still recall this."

It seemed to her that her mother-in-law had drawn circles of restraints around her. Being confined to those guidelines and restrictions, she had to worship and meditate. She should chant only the 'Omkar sound'. There will be no earthly desire there.

Since that day, she had a blended feeling of fear and devotion for her mother-in-law. Her outer appearance and indifference doubled her personality. She was lean and thin in physique; because of her mortal body's thick layer of spirituality, she seemed to be a female monk, a spiritual leader! This is how the mother-in-law appears to her eyes.

Even her daily Life is religion-based. She gets up early in the morning. She takes a quick bath near the well. After cleaning the *puja* room's utensils outside, she rubs the sandalwood on *pedi* (a specially designed stone). Then, she will continue worshipping in the *Thakur ghar* till 8 o'clock.

By that time, Sarita must have completed her routine work. She will serve her mother-in-law a plate of flattened rice, sugar, and a lump of grated/shredded coconut. After having breakfast, she will prepare herself for cooking. On the day when the smell of non-veg soup spread inside the house for Chiku's wrath, the mother-in-law was outraged and made separate arrangements for cooking her food. Later on, she no longer had any obsession with Chiku's happiness.

Her food items include a small measure of unboiled rice, a fistful of green gram, a raw banana and two potatoes. She will prepare *Khechudi* (a kind of mixed boiled/fried rice). When she seasons that *khechudi* with cow ghee, the scent of the dish spreads to many houses in the surrounding area.

After having lunch, mother-in-law will lie down in the afternoon for a while and wake up at four o'clock. Then, she will have a cup of ginger tea. After that, she will take care of the flower plants. If needed, she will pour water at the flower plants.

In the evening, she will change his clothes and sit to worship. Again, after eating the rest of *the khechudi* inside the cauldron, she will go to bed. If she finds a slight deviation in her routine work, she will roar, saying 'immoral conduct' everywhere.

The daily life of her mother-in-law inside the house is just like this, although various rumours about her are going on in the village.

Some say *Chari* Brahmin. She will not allow anyone's shadow to fall on her. Some say she is a miserly old lady!! Pilgrimage is a far-reaching concept for her. She never even visits Puri, the Jagannatha Dham, to observe *Habisya Vrat* in *Kartik* (October-November). Some say she is 'old-fashioned'. Coming of age and arriving on Mars, The old lady has grasped traditions and customs.

Debananda is the son of the mother-in-law who appears in two different forms at home and outside. Like his father-in-law, he is a devout Brahmin and an ethical person. He has accepted and approved some changes of time in life. That's why he doesn't like to comment outside his home. He has tried his best to make his mother-in-law comfortable. He has decided to go on a pilgrimage. Mother-in-law doesn't listen to him saying - 'What benefit will I get through pilgrimage? My God is not in those places: neither worshipped there nor in them.

She feels her father-in-law's soul inside the house. She has sheltered herself in the spiritual power that is limited and stationary in one place for her release from this worldly mire. The feet of the deity installed at their home are everything for her. For that, there is no need to visit Badrika.

Hence, Debananda never forces her mother.

How will Sarita believe the change in her mother-in-law's way of Life? If she said to Debananda, he argues that

'For so many years, one who has been practising austerity and is reformed. How can she behave like this? Man finds happiness in his etiquette and behaviour when he believes in God. My mother is a believer in God.'

Although not a great scholar in the scriptures, Sarita is intelligent. She can opine on different issues. She could interrupt Debananda by saying, 'Life is not a matter of taste. Its change is inevitable with time.

But she can't. She surrenders before Debananda not only for her husband but also for Debananda's scholarly and scriptural knowledge.

Sarita is with her endless thoughts.

The day has ended. The people are on evening walks. My daughter and daughter-in-law are ready to light the lamp before *chaura* (a raised platform with a basil plant). Her mother-in-law is *worshipping at Thakur Ghar*. It's time for Debananda to return.

The mother-in-law was meditating. Sarita wanted a decision and her release from all the internal conflicts. Otherwise, this conflict will become a headless living trunk and dance around her. And the doubts about the mother-in-law, like the prohibitions of the new moon day, would blacken and spread.

The mother-in-law has just left the worshipping place. She may not tell stories to Chikku this day. She tells stories to Chikku if she wants. The stories are 'The Old Female Demon', 'The King and Queen' etc. When Sarita sits near the hearth, she hears all those stories of her mother-in-law.

Sarita suddenly remembered a story told by her Mother-in-law that day. Why was she telling such stories? She understands this today.

The story was: 'There was a bird named after 'Burundi' living in a banyan tree. Though she had one stomach, she had two faces. She eats worms and insects in one mouth and fruits in the other. One day, there was a conflict between the faces; who was better? One said, I am vegetarian, so I am good. The other stated that I eat according to my taste and that I am good. The fight didn't end there. Burudi went to a saint. He answered: No matter what the food is or how it goes, it finally reaches the same stomach.

Sarita got confounded.

There was quite a connection between her mother-in-law's story and the incident of her tasting the non-veg soup.

Why was there such a change in her mother-in-law?

Is it for the sake of 'moksha' (salvation)?

While reading the *Bhagawat*, she repeatedly uttered the word '*Moksha*'.

The mother-in-law's transformation is from her pessimistic thoughts. What sort of '*moksha*' is achieved from negativity?

Sarita wouldn't have thought of this.

For some days, her mother-in-law was talking about '*moksha*'. She said '*moksha*' is not about cleansing the filthiness from mind and body. "*Moksha* is the transformation of mentality, wisdom, and antiquity."

Night has already deepened. There is complete silence everywhere. Mother-in-law's snoring sound is heard. We are not spirits but humans with flesh and blood.

Debananda has already returned.

Sarita served him food, and she also sat down to eat. They were almost finishing food. It's the right time to make any decision. Sarita said, "Do you know Mom has touched non-veg items today? She has also tasted the same. Now, there is no escape from its clutch. You know we are inviting significant trouble!!

Debananda was surprised to hear this and said, "How can I believe this?"

Sarita got irritated and said, "Am I telling you a lie?" How many times have I told you that Mom is losing her senses? You are not listening to me. Instead of holy books, Mom has developed an interest in watching television. She is hooked on the serials, which are full of stormy-naked pictures.

Moreover, she nowadays sits without blocking her ears and is engaged in gossiping in the neighbourhood. There is nothing good in whatever stories she tells to Chikku. A few days before she said the *Bhurunda* bird's story, what is in that story? Everything, whether good or bad, profit or loss, or veg or non-veg, is for human beings. But looking for a human character is not correct. Tell me what Chiku will learn from this!

Debananda got absorbed in thoughts.

He said, "Mom has not only focused on the sanctity of family tradition but also practised that mode of Life. How can I say her 'non-practitioner' of religious conduct?"

Silence spread in the house for some time. Her mother-in-law was sleeping peacefully. Sarita's sleepiness is another form of silence.

Debananda was looking towards his father's photo. In the father's demise, his black-framed photo is worshipped in place of *Thakura ghara*. He breathed heavily. When he said, his throat choked, "I was in my mother's womb while my father left for the other world. Since that day, his mom has lived a life of austerity and detachment, even though she is living in this mortal world. After our marriage and the birth of our son, Mom sees a full world. Maybe she is inclined towards delusion. This is the eternal truth: delusion comes from the world and then to salvation from delusion... And to return from salvation to delusion is only a sign of the unrighteousness."

You can't call mom 'dishonest', Sarita. The appropriate change is salvation, and improper change is sin.

Sarita could not say anything more. This lesson is mysterious, like the dead hour of night.

There were a few hours left for the night to end. Sarita's mind was fast, but not the night. Debananda was asleep deeply. Both waking and sleeping are like meditations for him.

Sarita fell asleep after some time. 'Sleep' is the best way to eliminate confusion. When I woke up, I had seen the sunlight outside the window. In the morning, the environment fills up the mind with freshness.

At this time, someone was knocking at the door. Sarita got up from the bed abruptly. She was not only waking up but was also waking up to a new life after the simple life of the past.

Sarita opened the chain of the door.

The one in front of her was not only her mother-in-law but a temple completely whitewashed.

Her body was white: a *rudraksha* (rosary) around the neck, sandalwood on the forehead, and a bag on her shoulder.

Sarita was stunned. She couldn't say anything. Without

letting her think anything more, her mother-in-law said, "I am going to Jagannath Dham, Puri, my daughter...?" Saying this, she was walking fast and gradually disappearing. Ahead is the Holy Dham...the Shrikshetra... Ahead is the Vrindaban...

Sarita turned around. Debanand was behind her... Her tear-soaked eyes were stretched far... By that time, my Mother-in-law had disappeared from the horizon!

THE STATUE OF GANDHI

In the house are three brothers. Except for Budhiram, all of them are vicious and cruel. Despite his name being Budhiram, all the brothers believe he is the most foolish. Blood-related, the brothers rise against him for various reasons. But while reprimanding, no distinction is made. They have a dialectical style of speech. Still, their hands are up. Budhiram remained silent. He is like *Daru...Brahma... Murari*. He sits in that posture.

Indumati supports her husband and ties her saree around her waist. On the other hand, one voice gets ready to battle when three voices yell simultaneously. Then, Indumati's voice fades away slowly. After that, she sits down and removes her clothing up to her waist. Buddhiram approaches her.

Looking at Buddhiram, Indumati says, "You are sitting there. They are scolding you so much that you are not saying anything. After saying this, Indumati can't control herself and cries bitterly. But Budhiram is not around to wipe Indumati's tears. Suddenly, he moves away somewhere else. No one can understand why Budhiram leaves so suddenly. Indumati herself not. The influence of the thunderbolt-like event lasts for several hours each day, and as time goes on, the house becomes peaceful, and everything gets normalized after one or two days. Then, Budhiram comes back. Who knows how he becomes aware of the situation?

Budhiram is the eldest among the four brothers. But in the eyes of other brothers, he is a disgrace. Budhiram is uneducated, not that the others are highly educated, but they feel proud that they have attended some classes! Budhiram always does household work, or else he will work outside. He works hard and never sits idly. His earning is from hand to mouth. The other three brothers have yet to work. However, they feel it is their right to move around with swagger. The family is neither together nor apart. Older parents tell Budhiram, "As an elder brother, you are responsible for looking after the family. They are now moving around doing nothing. They will come to the right path once they are married.

Budhiram says nothing. He didn't even consider why he would feed the others' stomachs alone. Instead, Indumati has repeatedly said, "Will you nourish them all? If God wants, we will be three out of two tomorrow morning. Then, tell me what will happen to our family and future. Even after hearing this from Indumati, he never gets startled by the possible paternity and remains silent. Indumati tries to understand him from his twinkling eyes. However, she can't.

Budhiram indeed says nothing, but he is not dumb. He stays silent when it comes to family or his world. The rest of the time, he becomes talkative. He also has friends in the village with whom he jokes. On the ways and the bathing ghats, if he meets people, he interacts with them well. In today's politics, he never interferes, but he has the patience to listen to that attentively. If needed, he nods his head positively. When any discussion is at his house, he never says anything. No one understands this, not even Indumati, who had chosen him as his companion of happiness and sorrow.

That day, Indumati spoke in such a manner that Budhiram was forced to open his mouth. Opening his mouth does not mean that he has said something harshly. It is said that a man who lives silent for twenty hours at home has uttered a word. Considering this, neither Budhiram nor Indumati in the house ever thought such a big issue would happen.

Indumati said, "Where have you been since morning? Do you know when the sun rose and descended on the horizon?"

Today, Budhiram opens his mouth a little to answer Indumati again. He said, "Now it is the summer season. Farmland soil is stretched hard. If you plough a little, the soil will turn upside down. The inner soil will get the sunlight. Ploughing on the rainy season will be easy."

After hearing this from Budhiram, Indumati remained silent for a while. She expressed annoyance, saying, "You will work hard 24/7, while others will wander with pomp and vigour, having food at home and without doing anything."

Let them move as much as they can. When they get to work, they will know whether the fruit of wandering is sweet or sour! Budhiram answered this much.

Great! After listening to this, who will manage these three brothers? They cried out and said, "Lo, look, one who could not speak anything started saying boldly for her woman/wife.

"What did you say? We will become workless. We will not work hard in the farmland nor sweat and bleed like you."

They also said, "You think of yourself; we will think about us."

Indumati anticipated this conversation between the younger brothers and the elder brother. Three younger brothers did not annoy Indumati by raising their hands or making scathing remarks towards his husband. To expect all this from those who lack respect in society is pointless.

Indumati was afraid that he would go somewhere again. After all the trouble, he generally leaves the house and goes somewhere!

The person has returned home after working hard in the field. He has yet to take water; who is asking about bathing and eating? Indumati rushes straight to the house to call her in-laws. They will convince Budhiram and tell him not to leave the house. If he steps out, they will stop. That day, they didn't say anything to him, as if they were asleep or like a statue like Lord Vishnu.

Being hopeless from her in-laws, when Indumati returned, she saw Budhiram was not on the porch. She lost her moral courage. She sobbed bitterly, unable to control herself this time and declared, "This is my misfortune. I'm unlucky. That is happening with me, what I always fear."

If Buddhiram is with Indumati, even if he doesn't say anything, she finds her moral courage to quarrel with her brothers-in-law. She dares to tell them something. With her remaining strength, she pulled her leg out of the house. Slowly, she stepped forward. She asked the one she met on the way, "Have you seen Budhiram?" When everyone refused, she became imbalanced and hopeless.

Even the sun on the western horizon had scattered its crimson colour around. The sound of the chirping birds sitting on the tree branches was also slowly diminishing. People who like to walk outside the village have started stepping on the road outside the village. The small forest in the vicinity looked dark from time to time.

For a long time, Indumati couldn't wait for Budhiram to return. Even in the house, everything looked black and bleak to her tearful eyes. She didn't eat either. Her stomach started aching because she did not have food. At first, she thought she would go far to search. If nothing happened, she would dig into the forest.

Indumati remembered, "One day, she told Buddhiram that she would follow him. Buddhiram told her not to make such a mistake and that I will return to you over time. Remembering this, Indumati sat down suddenly under a tree and did not go any further.

Waiting for him for some time there, Indumati returned home. But the vibe is different at home. Sitting at the house, they all appear to have successfully driven a useless fellow away from home and passed pointless taunting. When Indumati entered the mansion, she immediately desired everything, even how she would part. The mother-in-law and father-in-law were positioned, as if in the region of Kurusabha, like Dhutarastra and Gandhari. They were unable to free themselves from that.

Running to the bedroom was Indumati. She wiped as many tears from her eyes as there were. Those tears left a smear on the pillow. Her anguish was still fresh in her mind.

Indumati thought Budhiram had left home many times. Her heart was troubled; she had overcome that with the pain. But why has an unknown fear tormented her today? She felt suffocation everywhere.

She has a little hope and faith that Buddhiram will return home someday. Indumati thought that way.

So, where does Buddhiram go? To this day, this question remains unsolved in Indumati's heart. There was no moment when she did not feel Buddhiram's footsteps coming. She never slept any day without searching for her husband on the village roads. Even if this did not happen, the five family members, including the mother-in-law and father–in–law, raised the issue of Buddhiram or became anxious about his arrival.

But Budhiram didn't come back. Days after days passed. Indumati's thoughts gradually transformed into questions, "What will she do now? Where will she go? Will she wait for him or search for him? If she goes, where will she go?"

This time, Indumati surrendered to her brothers-in-law for help. 'Your brother has gone missing; please find him.' But they had laughed at her like a villain on the opera stage. All her hopes were ruined at that sight. She begged her father and mother-in-law and requested. She reminded them that 'Your son has gone missing. Without hesitation, her father and mother-in-law said, 'He will not come! How often has this happened, or is it a new thing today?'

Indumati could not wait anymore. When Buddhiram didn't come for many days, many negative thoughts touched her mind. But a little hope, wait for her husband; the points of the mind making her fresh were being jarred in disbelief. Buddhiram's simple, innocent, and handsome body, which had been around for so long since marriage, was slowly becoming a shadow. Buddhiram was dim and indistinct in Indumati's teary eyes.

The sun had not yet risen at that time. The breeze of the summer morning was chilling the body. But Indumati was sweating and was running continuously.

Someone said, "Buddharam always sits on the bank of a stream flowing through the forest for a long time. Indumati reached the stream. The drops of tears from her eyes have become an ocean. Why would she look at her with tears in her eyes? Indumati was disappointed because she didn't find Buddhiram on the bank of the stream."

Another one said, "Buddhiram always sits on the branch of a thick tree in the forest. If asked why he sits there, he doesn't reply to anyone. If called, neither comes down. Indumati saw that a bird had a nest in the branch of a tree. Mother Bird is enjoying the chirping of her baby birds. Indumati returned from the place."

So, where did Buddhiram go? People usually don't go to the forest. There are no animals in the forest. It is the silence that often scares people. This silence in the forest is not suitable for a woman like her. She couldn't understand what to do next. "Do I still search more in the forest or return home?" Indumati started walking inexorably.

At the time, a man walks through the woods. Indumati knew that he was not from his village.

Indumati asked the stranger, "Did you see a person going that way?"

The man said, "No, I haven't. But I saw a dead person floating in the water."

Indumati was shocked, and her heartbeats increased, "Is that person not Buddhiram?" She ran to that side. The person was facing downward on the water. She wondered if he was Buddhiram or someone else. With great courage, she turned the man over. After that, she was relieved and thanked God. However, she could not get the fear out of her mind. She thinks, what if Buddhiram commits suicide because he cannot bear the scolding of his brothers? In the sorrows of a defeated man?

And she thought, didn't he commit suicide outside the forest? She was very much disturbed and imbalanced. This time, she started running madly in the forest. If she doesn't get Budhhiram, she will go back home, wait for the coming of Buddharam, and pray to God. Indumati thought, "If he does not return, she will hold on to life for whom?" She would come to this forest and commit suicide.

Indumati had seen all over the forest walking along

the riverbank; she fell again here but didn't find Buddhiram. Tears shed continuously from her eyes. She had walked into the forest expecting Buddhiram, but now she was in despair.

What option does Indumati have but to return home? She knows how much pain she must bear when she returns home. At that time, the pair of eyes of assurance would not be with Buddhiram to extend his life.

Indumati had already ventured into the road outside the jungle, along with the trees. Her mind was filled with internal conflicts while reaching the square. Will she come home or locate Buddhiram nearby? Will she go to the other side of the street?

Indumati was abruptly reminded that she had no idea when Buddhiram would cross the jungle. People moved on from their conversations, but she headed for the weekend market.

Indumati remembers Buddhiram going towards the market. Even if there is no work, he comes out of the house saying he is going to the market. A faint glimmer of hope flickered in Indumati's eyes. She must walk three kilometres from there. Indumati thought that no matter how hard it was, she had to find Buddhiram.

When Indumati reached the market, she saw people gathered outside. Indumathi was very thirsty; she didn't even have the energy and strength to find Buddhiram in the crowd. There was a tube well next to her. After gulping down the water, her body began to feel better. Sitting in the hut, she thought, "Is a meeting happening here?" When the crowd breaks up, she will get a chance to find Buddhiram.

At that time, someone's voice was afloat in the mic and echoed in Indumati's ears repeatedly.

'Today is Gandhi Jayanti. Gandhi, the father of our

nation, once said, "The greatest answer to anger is silence." Gandhiji also used to say that our relations depend on four points: (1) To respect each other, (2) To understand each other, (3) To accept each other, and (4) To be kind to all.

Indumati was shocked because the speech matched the incidents at her home.

After some time, the meeting was over. Indumati was looking for Buddhiram among the passersby. But she did not find that Buddhiram was among them. After being disappointed, Indumati was shedding her tears.

A short distance away from her is a platform. Indumati saw a strange man coming down from the platform; varnish or something was shining all over that person's body. He had a staff in his hands. He was walking towards her in a daze. Indumati was terrified at his get-up. She looked around hopelessly. No one was there after the meeting; there was silence all around.

As Indumati started to run from there, she came face-to-face with the man. She saw that the man was looking at her calmly, not afraid of her, not even a bit of movement.

She was unable to see him. There was no movement at all. Indumati thought, "Has she ever seen such a statue?" She remembered a face like this in the book while studying in school. He is Mahatma Gandhi. He is the father of our nation. So, why is this man dressed like him? She was not able to understand.

When Indumati raised her face and looked at him, she saw that he was also looking at her. This time, she got scared, and Buddhiram's face floated before her eyes. He would have appeared to save her!

Then, as she ran away, someone was calling her name. Indumati!

Indumati!!

Indumati!!!

Indumati was shocked.

Indumati: Who is in front of me, Gandhiji or Buddhiram??

Indumati calmed down after a while. After that, tears flowed from her eyes.

That person also walked very close. Indumati finally said, "Here is the strength to bear the pain."?

The idol man's countenance revealed a hint of humour upon hearing this.

Neither Gandhiji nor Buddhiram laughed. Indumati was slightly confused but then walked after the varnish-coloured idol man.

SATICHAURA

"Daddy, I have acquired a small piece of land in Cuttack."

Small plot? What does that mean? The land cost in the village has become exorbitant, making it unaffordable for us. Your purchase in Cuttack is a commendable achievement. What three generations couldn't accomplish, you have. You've made my life worthwhile!"

"But?"

"But what more? You may have thought I wouldn't question your decision after three generations, but couldn't you have freed the mortgaged land then? Was the decision to buy the land right? Not at all. The aspirations of a person and the flow of a river are always in the same direction. The river wants to move forward, and man wants to ascend. Father, climbing and moving forward are synonymous. Don't worry; what you've done is correct.

You instructed me to arrange money to release our land a few days ago. You emphasized that I should secure funds by any means necessary, even if it meant bringing money from your workplace in times of need. When I inquired about the amount, you told me to arrange two lakh rupees for the land release. You advised me to manage it according to my capacity. So, I will do my best."

However, today, the call with Bijan ended abruptly

when his father's phone disconnected. Despite repeatedly saying hello, there was no response. Bijan found himself in a quandary, uncertain whether his last words reached his father. He wished his father had heard his final words to understand his intentions. He redialed his father to confirm this, only to find the phone switched off.

Contemplating whether his father's happiness stemmed from the news about the land, Bijan struggled to discern his father's genuine emotions. The phone's abrupt disconnection left him wondering if it was intentional or an automatic glitch. Adding to his confusion, his father had yet to inquire about the financial arrangements for the land purchase. Bijan quickly questioned the acquired Cuttack land and pondered whether it involved borrowed money. The complexity of deciphering someone else's mindset contributed to the turmoil in Bijan's mind. He realized the dilemma might persist as a sealed box of his father's thoughts. This uncertainty left Bijan restless, anticipating that the unease would continue until his father shared his perspective. The prospect of the unknown response to the question he had hoped to ask his father terrified Bijan.

Bijon's occupation revolves around a prolonged cot in the vegetable storage facility at Chhatrabazar. Placed on this cot is a tool, and atop the tool rests a luggage collection. From this spot, he meticulously tracks the movement of goods transported by trucks from one location to another. The job is carried out manually but is expected to transition to computerized processes. The question arises: what are the prospects for his employment when that transition occurs, and what is the remuneration he receives for his services? What remains as his surplus income after deducting rent and living arrangements expenses?

Everyone envisions his salary like a pied-crested cuckoo—can he consistently remit it every month? Is it feasible to do so regularly? Occasionally, Bijon resorts to overtime, working seven or eight extra days a month, achieved through toil from morning until noon. He sends money home after earning some additional income through these efforts; otherwise, it remains uncertain how much he can contribute.

Bijon questions himself, trying to determine where the money used to buy the land came from. His mind is in such disarray that he contemplates skipping work, yet the persistent sound of the truck appears to beckon him. Despite his reluctance, he feels compelled to go. The necessity to earn a daily wage overrides his mental hesitations, and the fear of potential job loss looms if he skips work. This realization terrifies him.

Upon reaching Chhatrabazar, a bustling market, he encounters a heavy crowd. While this congestion might suffocate some, it brings joy to Bijan. He views this crowd as a boundary—one delineating the limits of life and another defining the world. He believes that the growth of the owner's business aligns with the crowd's pace, bringing benefits to employees like him. Furthermore, he contemplates the fixed boundaries of Odisha or India, recognizing that disputes over permanent boundaries stem from either positive or negative endeavours. However, the population of a stable continent is not stagnant; it is rapidly increasing. As he contemplates the disparity between those with minimal living space and those with extensive properties, Bijon envisions the necessity of uncontrolled crowds like the one in Chhatrabazar to counterbalance the pride associated with the land of Nitei Santara.

During idle moments at work, Bijan uses a green dot pen to sketch a river. When he revisits this drawing the next day, the image captivates him. The river depicted is the Gobari, which flows through his village. Adjacent to this river lies a small piece of land he owns, where crops grow. However, the produce from his land ultimately finds its way to the Niyteisantara garden.

Niteisantara, the clan that held sway over Bijon's village during the British era and continued to exert influence since independence, is now represented by its successor. Despite the passage of time, both his father's age and Nityeisantara's age have increased. The landscape remains unchanged, with the land benefiting from increased fertility due to alluvial deposits. However, the burden of the loan against the mortgaged land has significantly escalated, now amounting to two lakhs.

Reflecting on this, Bijon inadvertently adds five zeros after two when writing the figure. When alerted, he crosses it over to correct the error. Given the nature of Bijon's work, even a slight lapse or a single-digit alteration is viewed as a significant mistake. Whether this mistake results in profit or loss is a separate matter, but there is no leniency for such errors. Despite correcting the digit with his pen, Bijon still senses the lingering impact of that digit, akin to a mark on the land near the river, resembling a dot on a dice.

He thought about their clan's successive patriarchs, my great-grandfather, grandfather, and father. He could not recall seeing his great-grandfather's father, the ancestor of their family, but he could visualize his great-grandfather as a guy made of flesh, bones, and blood. Situated near his father and Niteisantara, the land connected to the Sanatra Clan dates back to his great

grandfather's era, which has changed over time.

It was recounted that his great-grandfather was skilled in playing dice. Whether in the past or the present, dice games involve wagers. Unfortunately, his great-grandfather lost in one such dice game, resulting in the mortgaging of the land to Santara Saheb. Although the era of British rule has ended, the tradition of addressing him by his name, "Saheb", persists. Not only in his village and among the residents of three neighbouring hamlets, he was recognized as Santara.

Saheb. During that period, an agreement was made that he would return the property if his great-grandfather repaid the loan. While he could cultivate the land, he would not be required to pay interest on the loan amount.

However, the task of repaying the money proved challenging for his great-grandfather. Consequently, the land remained mortgaged, and without the release of the land, his great-grandfather passed away. The vegetables cultivated on that land near the river ended up in Santara Saheb's possession, contributing to the contents of his stomach. At the same time, the proceeds from the sale went into his pocket.

My grandfather displayed some irrational and unintelligent behaviour during his younger years. At that time, the thought of releasing the mortgaged land did not cross his mind. This was a reflection of his youth. Once, in a fit of anger, he visited the residence of Bhagyadhar Santara, the son of Santra Saheb, who had already passed away.

Bhagyadhar Santara explained to him that he had honoured the commitment made by his father, keeping the land mortgaged as per the handwritten agreement from his father. On the contrary, as the successor, he was responsible for upholding the truth by releasing the land.

While his great-grandfather was involved in dice games, his grandfather struggled with opium addiction. Intoxicated individuals may express anger but often carry the weight of their failures. Despite continuous efforts, his grandfather could not release the land. It was believed that he had somehow extracted a promise from my father to free the land, ensuring the peace of his great -grandfather's soul. Eventually, his grandfather passed away.

His father persisted in stressing the value of the land after his grandfather's death. It was more than a piece of real estate; to him, it was the spirit of three generations. Reaching out to the river, his father would often say, "The river aims to flow ahead." Humanity's work is progressing. We will move forward when this land comes back to us.

Daddy doesn't say. He looks at the land and cultivates a dream. If that...!!! Father said, ' If we get rid of this land, I will grow crops on it. I will get a lot of money by selling it in the market, and we won't have any scarcity. '

On that land, Nitei Santara cultivates fruit. After the death of Bhagyadhara Santara, the fortune of this land is now in the hands of Nitei Santara. Father could not bear it after seeing this fruit. But, he would need more resources to redeem. If there is no resource, there is no way.

Father always asks one thing, 'can I get rid of that land? I can keep my promise to my father in my lifetime. Can I or can't I? '

After arriving at Nitei Santara, "Hold on, I will now take back our land," he remarked to him. What is the current amount I have to pay? He declared that the land should now be paid for with two lakh rupees and levied compound interest.

Father felt that someone was picking him up. Where are two lakh rupees? Who is he? As he has no more land, he brings land and cultivates vegetables. In this soil, vegetables are more productive than paddy or rabi crops. That's why people are more interested in vegetable farming. The money from selling the veggies at the market must be increased to provide food for the five family members. Where can he obtain the two lakh rupees required to grant the land?

After witnessing Father's desperation for the land, Bijan muses: could the land lose its revenue as the home gradually disappears into the water? Does it take place? Then, neither he nor Nitei Santara would own the land! If the land disappears, the father can relieve much pain. At last, he was cursing nature for not speaking. Subsequently, he captured the Nitei Santara leader and loaded him with stones. Why is all of his lush, productive land protected? The abstraction came to an end.

The landslide stopped descending as soon as the stones were piled. Bijan is bothered by his father's constant yelling, "Land, land." "My father, how can I miss the harvested land?" the father said as he walked. That is intolerable to me! Father, the soul of your grandfather will depart.

Spirit?

It is spinning all the time. You don't see him about the house on a night like this. But that spirit's power is driving Father insane.

His father told him, "Anyway, we have to release the land," four days before he received the news. I'm not feeling well these days. Who is to determine when and what will occur? He could not pass away in peace if he could not free the land by gathering two lakh rupees. It will shatter my spirit.

Bijan needed help to answer this. I couldn't. Can I collect so much money? I can't say that that's why those words might hurt the father so hard that he won't be able to get up.

He took some time from his father. The truth is, what he was that even if he could not pay the money, his father would never have been hurt; he was worried about that when he said that he bought the land today after hearing that Bijan could not understand the extent of his father's happiness.

It was Bijan's way of thinking; he had yet to learn how long the paper had been written. Two lakhs. Just that. He was taken aback by the boss's outburst and realized what had happened.

What is this calculation, the boss yells incessantly? quadrilateral diagram. Two hundred thousand rupees. Are you having trouble thinking?

Bijan said, "You can give me two lakh rupees, sir," suddenly.

The owner looked at him. Then he shouted, two lakhs? Am I running a bank here, or what? How many months will I have to go without salary if I take two lakh rupees? Three years, four months!! I will tell you whether you have made a mistake today, whether I will keep it or not. '

The owner was roaring like that. I was surprised to find out when he reached Bijan's room. It was ten o'clock at that time. He was exhausted. The room is like a small house. Where the dark, hide-and-seek game continues, just like his life. Today, it seemed as if darkness was coming into his life. When he took the phone out of his pocket, his father called three times. So late at night, father called!!!

There was even a ring when he called, and his younger brother picked up the phone. The younger brother said, 'Something is happening to father's chest. He can't handle it. I will take him to Cuttack tomorrow. It would help if you were on leave. '

Leave?

Bijan burst into tears. Do you hold hands like this when it's terrible?

Bijan had not slept at night. Every minute and second of the night, the ticking sound of pain was burning her heart like a throne. He had grown up in order not to grow up. He could not grow up because of the compulsion to grow up.

He did not know when the night had passed and the morning had come.

By nine o'clock, his younger brother had caught up with his father. The father's body had deteriorated entirely. Father was not saying anything; he was looking at him unthinkingly. But there were many things in that look that Bijan could understand.

The Doctor said, 'High blood pressure and severe heart problem!! You never know what will happen?' He also said it's better to do the operation quickly.

Bijan asked very seriously, 'Operation? how much will it cost?' The Doctor said, 'Two lakhs!!! '

Two lakhs!!!

Bijan was shocked. There is a single word that alerts the subconscious mind of a confused person. 'Two lakh rupees 'echoed in his father's ear repeatedly. He said in a hoarse voice, 'two lakhs'. I do not need an operation. He has bought that place now; where will he get the money for the operation? '

Father was sleeping in the medical bed. Bijan was moving inside and outside the medical centre as if every foot of his chest trembled. Fear reigns over every face and every moment. It would have broken into pieces if it had been a natural hill.

He does not know how long the night will be by then. Bijan used to rest his head on his father's bed while sitting down. Meanwhile, his father's hand was on his body. Father was probably calling him. He got up and looked at his father's face.

Father's voice is coming in faint. Father said, don't worry about me; I already know I don't have more time.

As Bijan was crying, father said, 'Don't cry. I am not sad even if I am gone. But, I was left with one regret. I could not get rid of the land while I was alive. I know you can't release it today. You will remove the land tomorrow.

But, the father is holding one happiness and leaving. You have bought a piece of land in Cuttack. '

Two drops of tears fell from the corner of the father's eyes. Bijan could no longer support himself. Cried. Father slowly raised his hand and wiped the tears from his eyes. And he said, 'Are you sad for the land! It is not released today; it will be released tomorrow. I always say water moves forward like that man wants to grow and move forward. What is the price of the land purchased from our land in Cuttack? When everyone in the village heard it, they said you must have done a great job and be getting a good salary. After hearing this, I was thrilled. I was so happy that I couldn't contain myself. Maybe God could not bear my happiness. Since then, I have chest pain. Oh....... What is suffering. '

Bijan cried a lot and asked: 'Where do I buy the money for the land? Won't you ask me, father? '

Father said: 'Where did you buy the money for the land? What do I know? I don't have the patience to hear the price of the place you bought, son. There is no more time. You know, where your grandfather used to bring the land and keep it tied up, today it has reached two lakhs. So, the value of space is not seen, its size is seen, and its ownership is seen. You see, even if it is our land, its owner is another! '

After talking for so long, the father was getting steamed up. No matter how much Bijan refused, he did not listen. Father, who was in pain, asked in that state: 'Which place you bought the land? Can you show me a bit? You see, after seeing your place, I can die peacefully. Where is that place? Shall I be taken now? '

Bijan was shocked. Suddenly, Satichaura came out of his mouth. 'Satichaura!!!'

Father looked at Bijan with wide eyes. He said, 'Satichaura, where a person dies and is burnt, that place!! Well, you will burn me when I am dead. '

Bijan burst into tears. Father's eyes were closed. Even his nose was becoming shallow. Then, as much as pain his father had, it seemed to Bijan that he would burn. Satichaura! In that small place of yours is the abode of many dead. His father's body was burnt there. In that fire, Bijan himself was burnt to ashes.

SEALING WAX

'Dhrutarastra was born blind. He couldn't visualize the physical world. He did not even have divine knowledge. But Sanjay used to tell Dhrutarastra about the minute details of the Mahabharata war with his divine power'.

As it said earlier, 'Set a thief to catch a thief.' An argument needs a counter-argument. That's why Pradyumna delivered this aphorism. He thought Mrutyunjay would remain silent this time. Otherwise, his so-called philosopher's mind will stir with this thought.

But Mrutyunjaya was already prepared. He immediately said, 'Sanjay did not gain divine knowledge by his practice and efforts! When Dhrutarastra prayed for him to know about the details of Mahabharata, Vyasa blessed Sanjay with this boon of divine power. What is the significance of gaining any accidental result by others without experiencing the life test personally?'

Pradyumna was speechless. During their childhood, both of them used to study together in school. Together, they went to college as well. Coincidentally, both got jobs in the same college. The two have already spent fifty years together with each other. However, Sanjay couldn't win over Mrutyunjay's argument.

Sanjay is always satisfied with his inability to win over

Mrutyunjay's argument. This inability never pierced into his chest, being a thorn, nor did it turn into a volcano.

Pradyumna loves Mrutyunjay immensely. He loves his craziness much more than his friend. He also loves his deep relationship with life.

Materials need testing: poison for Socrates and jump into the unfathomed sea for Dharmapada. Surprisingly, Mrutunjay himself will become an instrument for testing in the laboratory! He will stay strong and drink poison like Socrates without any fear of death or will jump into the bottom of the sea like Dharmapada as a saviour to the lives of twelve hundred sculptors. But he would never surrender his life. It is said that many people carry the burden upon other's shoulders. They take advantage of the situations, using others as their weapons. They present themselves only, keeping others aside. At least Mrutyunjay is not on that list.

'What kind of thought are you absorbed in, now?'

He questions Mrutunjay. This time, Pradyumna looks at him once.

The eyes are blindfolded. He wears a pair of loose trousers and a sleeveless vest. One can book a cabin in a nursing home for a small amount. But these days, getting admitted into government hospitals is a nightmare. If there are cabins, these are reserved only for the rich. Pradyumna glanced at the house and said the cabin was ten by ten square feet tall, with artificially painted walls and coated white everywhere. A standing fan is found at one end of the bed, while a tool is at the other. A water bottle, a doctor's prescription, and medicines are found there.

Seeing him silent, Mrutyunjay asks him once again. Are you going home? Who knows what the time at night is? How long have I been telling you to go home and leave me alone for a while? You don't listen, nor do you move! You know well that it's the most important day of my life.

Pradyumna seemed to laugh at his madness but kept silent, thinking of something else. This Mrutyunjay can't say what time at night it is as he is blindfolded and will understand the principles of life in one night, for which the sages had undergone meditation for years.

These days, the corporate world arranges meditation and yoga centres. Greenery and accessible space for Nature are not needed for this. If one can control worldly desires, the healthy thoughts in the mind will ingrain naturally. And if one wants to prove that meditation culminates in enlightenment, a white air-conditioned building is enough. And there is no need to visit any region of Aryavrat because, now, in the battle between the artificial and the natural, the influence of the artificiality is felt more. The natural state is on the verge of extinction.

Today, in a room like the earlier ambience, Mrutyunjay will subdue all the senses. He will give a test that he is self-restraint. Self-abnegation will be mastered. He will control all his desires. He will experience the true 'Philosophy of Life'. He will discern the mysteries of creation with his divine eyes.

Mrutyunjay is blindfolded under this pretext. Whoever hears this should take him straight to a psychiatrist. However, Pradyumna has understood Mrutyunjay's mentality well. That is why he does not oppose or resist whatever he wants. Otherwise, his strange madness will appear again. If needed, he will leave home for months and reside elsewhere.

At that time, no one could trace his whereabouts. He will face the unknown fear of sisters-in-law Lucy and Mickey until Mrutyunjay is not searched for. He would be breathless, searching him.

Three months earlier, I felt very sad thinking about it. To me, my sister-in-law Lucy's innocent, tearful eyes were visible. Mickey's pale face filled his chest with melancholy.

That day, Mrutyunjay went to college and resigned from his job. Pradyumna was shocked to hear this. The quarters of Pradyumna are inside the college campus. It was close by, and he reached straight away.

Sister-in-law Lucy was sobbing. Mickey was also crying, embracing her. After seeing Pradyumna, Mrutyunjay said shamelessly, "I know you came here straight after hearing this."

Can anybody be happy with the job, the world and the give-and-take life? Can't we test the nitty gritty of our life with something else? Even without a job, a person can struggle and survive. Why can't I prove it, Pradyumna?

What would Pradyumna say to this mad? He knows he will be useless now if he says anything to him. People like Mrutyunjay, searching for the essence and the theoretical underpinnings of philosophy, will never accept others. What did Socrates receive? What will Mrutyunjay take? Pradyumna came back that day without uttering a single word to Mrutyunjay. The presence of Mrutyunjay had provided little courage to his sisters-in-law, Lucy and Mickey. By the time he came back, overwhelmed, Pradyumna had filled up with tears and started to cry like a victim of a terrorist attack or a train accident.

When he returned, Pradyumna looked at Mrutyunjay for a moment. He was Silent, speechless and motionless. On the way, Pradyumna thought, "Is this a man? Who speaks the words of philosophy but has no reaction in the mind. He is still and steady like a hill".

The next day, he heard that Mrutyunjay had gone somewhere. Sister-in-law Lucy said there was a face-off between the two until last night over resigning from the job. War meant here what sister-in-law Lucy wanted to say, said freely without any inhibition. Mrutyunjay, however, was in a state of complete silence. Then, both of them fell asleep. When she woke up, Mrutyunjay was not in his bed.

"Who will suffer? He would suffer?" thought Pradyumna.

Pradyumna knew that Mrutyunjay was crazy. He has tried to understand life flawlessly from his childhood days. He was also good at studies. However, he used to research something more that was not directly related to his studies.

Pradyumna was reminded of their childhood days. A sage came to visit the village that day. He had worn saffron-coloured clothes and sandalwood marks on his forehead. He had an oblong water pot held in his hand. Upon seeing him, Mrutyunjay started to follow him. Suddenly, there was a rumour in the evening that Mrutyunjay had gone somewhere with that sage. The next day, after searching him a lot, he was seen begging with that sage in a village ten kilometres away from his village. He insisted upon staying with the sage to seek the truth. It will lead him to peace after much understanding. He returned home.

Pradyumna calls Mrutyunjay's parents, who are elder fathers and elder mothers. Both of them are dead. Both of them were alive when they went to college together and were working together. They always said, "Hey, Pada (He addressed Pradyumna affectionately)... our son is mad." God gave a friend like you to assist him. Be there next to him, son; we can die in peace with that belief.

Mrutyunjay was likely for quite some years after marrying his sister-in-law, Lucy. He didn't bring anything absurd to his mind. Pradyumna felt relieved and thought that Mrutyunjay could handle himself now. At least his sister-in-law Lucy is there with him during the hard times.

But no changes are marked in him. He shows his lunacy once again.

Suddenly, he left home. Pradyumna restlessly looked for him everywhere. Finally, he found Mrutyunjay in an old home and brought him back. He came to know that he was cooking there. Mrutyunjay said, "The cycle of circumstances has brought these elderly people to shelter at this old-age home. Their home and relatives are now unknown to them. Now, they are the beings left

alone on the earth. There is pain and struggle, but they still want to live their lives. I have come to this place to understand the true meaning of life."

Pradyumna didn't know whether to be angry at his madness or laugh at his deeds.

Pradyumna brought Mrutyunjay back home with incredible difficulty. He resigned from the job and disappeared once again. After searching, Pradyumna found him at a nursing home. He was blindfolded. Seeing that Pradyumna was silent, Mrutyunjay asked, "Are you here, or have you left? Pradyumna didn't utter a word; hence, Mrutyunjay thought that Pradyumna had left. But, at this moment, Pradyumna coughed; listening to this, Mrutyunjay growled. Hey, you are sitting here? How often have I called you, and you don't even respond? What's stuffed in your mouth?" This time,

Mrutyunjay forced him away because of his apprehension of being late.

Tonight, he will stay alone. He doesn't permit both Lucy and Mickey to be in that condition. He has warned them not to come to the nursing home.

Then, Pradyumna came out from there. Mrutyunjay indulged in his thoughts so much that he forgot to say 'goodnight' out of courtesy.

Outside the Nursing home, the road is narrow. The shutters of most of the shops have already been pulled down. And the shutters of some shops are half open. A few medicine shops are open because the nursing home is nearby. After all, the lights of the shops are switched off; the street lights are also affected. The street dogs have slowly started coming up to the road.

Pradyumna stood on the street for a while, waiting for an auto to reach College Street. The quarters are a few steps away. Of course, after ten O'clock at night, the college road feels dreary. But no unexpected is likely to happen. So he can go without fear.

Pradyumna waited for ten minutes. At this time, his mobile rang. He took it out of his pocket and saw 'Home Calling'.

When are you coming? It is half past ten.

Just returning.

Pradyumna was about to hang up the call.

His wife's voice was coming from the other side of the phone.

Hey, listen to me! Are you waiting to receive any parcels? Someone from the courier office had called and wanted to know where our house was.

Parcel!.. I am trying to remember. All right, I'm coming.

Pradyumna started to think about the parcel. Any auto had yet to arrive. It will be challenging to find a car late at night. He hopes to find an automobile as several nursing homes are nearby. That is why he is waiting. If not, how long will it take to reach? He is one and a half kilometres away from the campus.

No auto reached there. Pradyumna started walking without waiting any more.

While walking, he tried to remember again: Where did this parcel come from? He did not order!! He indeed wanted to order some reference books. But he has just posted the request letter. So, where did this parcel come from?

Pradyumna remembered while walking. A few days ago, Mrutyunjay said he had ordered some spiritual books in his name. A book is in it -'Divine Vision and Divine Consciousness'. He also said: 'Tell me about it after reading.'

Pradyumna was irritated and said, "Where is the time to read all these absurd books?" With preparation, one will be able to take the honours class. That is why the books of various authors are being followed. And sometimes you have to write a note and dictate it. Apart from this, two scholars are also pursuing Ph. D. under my supervision. Among the two, the girl will leave for America in December after her marriage. Before that, she had to complete and submit the thesis. I don't have time to read these religious books for you?"

"How will you be benefitted from all these books?" asked Pradyumna.

Mrutyunjay got up and refuted, "Hey, don't lecture too much." If you like, read it; otherwise, don't. These books are for you. You don't have to pay for them or even the courier cost. These books are available free of charge. Only a letter is to be sent to receive them.

While saying this, Mrutyunjay was getting a bit emotional. He said: This book is the medicine to the confusion created in the human mind, about truth and lies, light and darkness and rise and fall of beings. Looking at Pradyumna, Mrutyunjay said again: 'Alas! How silly people are. Even if it's available free of cost, it's hard for people to accept!'

At this time, an auto horned from behind. Pradyumna stopped and asked for a lift by raising his hand. The auto was reserved; it didn't stop.

Pradyumna continued with his walk. Almost half a kilometre is covered; one more kilometre to go. It's not yet eleven. One will be a bit scared if it's past twelve. One will have to face the nuisance of the street Romeos along with street dogs.

Pradyumna thought of Mrutyunjay. What a strange mentality! Sometimes, he would go to some monastery after becoming a monk.

When Pradyumna observes Mrutyunjay's behaviour, he thinks that he won't be able to become a monk. All these are his madness because he is a non-vegetarian. He wears the same attire as he used to dress up earlier. But while speaking, it only feels like he is 'hypnotized' by the third sense.

A doctor friend of Pradyumna used to say: The symptoms that Mrutyunjay shows are of 'Anxiety Disorder'. These erupt from any 'phobia'. He can be cured by 'psychotherapy'. But did he hear? He reached out to the 'ophthalmologist.

Two days earlier, Mrutyunjay suddenly appeared near

College Street and started saying absurd things. Between these conversations, he suddenly said. ..What if I become blind?

This is a bizarre question. When asked this question, Mrutyunjay was absorbed in his thoughts again.

Breaking his silence, Pradyumna said: 'What else will happen? You destroyed the life you had built with your hands and finished whatever little was left. You will die yourself and won't go without killing the other two.

None of Pradyumna's words affected Mrutyunjay. Suddenly, he disappeared from that place. Today, suddenly, sister-in-law Lucy gave a call and said Mrutyunjay was admitted to the nursing home and his eyes were to be operated on. He has been saying since yesterday that his eyes have been itching. Pradyumna couldn't wait and rushed immediately after completing the class. It was a lovely evening, but he was blown away by whatever he heard from the doctor. There was no problem in the eye. It turned a little red. An eye drop would cure it. But he is adamant that he must be blindfolded for this night."

In this one night, he will gain divine vision. The layers of life that lie hidden in the senses of his knowledge will be illuminated before him in his quest for life. He will explore the secret of life!

Huh... one night!

' Pradyumna was about to laugh. In this one night, he will understand the secret of life. When asked, he said He has been examining his life for many days. So, the vision he will gain differs from the result of one night.

Instead, it is "A golden moment".

Very strange!

Thinking these things, Pradyumna had already reached College Street. At this point, he looked back. He saw an auto coming at high speed suddenly, gave a brake, and asked if he would go ahead. Pradyumna shook his head and said, "Annoyingly". These autos don't appear when needed but come over when not needed. He didn't sleep well at night. He felt anxious while thinking about Mrutyunjay's childhood, his deceased great-father, great-mother, and sisters-in-law, Lucy and Mickey. He also thought about the strange things about him and the nursing home. All these thoughts leave his mind in a state of mess.

Suddenly, he seemed startled. He woke up quickly, sat down, and thought: what if Mrutyunjay creates some mischievous deed at night, or if he goes somewhere?

He perspired upon such thoughts. Looking at Pradyumna's condition, his wife said: "You think all these unnecessarily. Is this something new for him? She asks him to sleep peacefully, but he cannot sleep or get rid of his thoughts. He was waiting for the day to break, and he would immediately rush to the nursing home, but the dawn was yet to come. Pradyumna was lying on the bed with only his eyes closed but fully active and conscious. He often felt that someone was knocking at the door. And it seemed as if the phone were ringing. With all these incidents happening, Pradyumna did not know it was already morning: the sound of the sweeper's hooting outside and the horning of cars on the road signalled morning arrival. Nowadays, not even one can hear the crow's cawing anymore. It is not heard in the village; how can one expect from the city?

Pradyumna had already gotten up from bed and was ready. He thought of reaching the Nursing home by walking.

The college campus is adjacent to his quarters; hence, it is within walking distance.

Pradyumna went through that path without taking any other way. Then he reached the college. A promenade stretches up to the college gate, touching the main road. Another lane of staff quarters lies on the right side of the college road. Among them, Mrutyunjay owns one. Even though he resigned from his job, the principal did not accept his resignation. Hence, legally, he did not leave the service, nor did he leave the college quarters. Mrutyunjay's door was closed. Who knows in what condition sister-in-law Lucy and Mickey will be in?

Upon reaching the Nursing home, whatever Pradyumna visualized made his legs cold. Mrutyunjay was not there in the cabin. Even the attendant could not say anything precisely where he went.

Blindfold is lying on the bed. The medicine strip is still on the table. But the water bottle is half finished.

"Where did Mrutyunjay go?"

The question was one, but there was numerous speculation about it. Various thoughts stirred Pradyumna's mind. Pradyumna thought: This time, perhaps Mrutyunjay has gone too far. For him, the house is like a wax house, and the outside world is like his own earth. It is the proper place to improve one's inner consciousness and thoughts. This time, he won't return home or be at home.

Mickey and Lucy's two innocent faces floated before Pradyumna's eyes this time. How scared! How sad!!

What will he answer them?

Thinking of this, Pradumna sat down quietly.

Now, facing these two people is more painful for Pradyumna than for Mrutyunjay.

At this time, his mobile rang. When he saw the phone, he found Mrutyunjay's family members calling him. The phone number was brightly shining on the screen. Pradyumna was startled. He got scared as well. He felt how much courage it takes to face a cruel truth. He asked himself whether to pick up the call, but in the meantime, the call got disconnected.

The phone rang once again. Pradyumna thought avoiding it would not be correct. What will the sister-in-law think? If Mickey were around, what would be her state of mind?

Sister-in-law Lucy would say: 'Don't I know what kind of man he is?' I have been through such an unknown tsunami, leaving some people feeling insignificant. Is there something new about this that you're afraid of when picking up my phone?'

Pradyumna was startled. He felt a little cold despite the dripping sweat on his body. When I answered the phone, it came floating from the other side…

'Good morning, Pradyumna'.

Hey! This is Mrutyunjay. He is at home now. After knowing this, an unspoken enthusiasm gradually spread over my body, creating a wave of excitement and curiosity. He thought: What could be more surprising than this?

This time, he returned to a normal state. Said: Hey, you have already reached home, and I am having trouble not finding you in the hospital. Give the phone to my sister-in-law Lucy.

'Talk to me first.'

'What nonsense are we going to talk about? I cannot listen to your nonsense and see your madness.'

'Listen to me once today, Pradyumna. I have got my divine vision. I am telling the truth.'

'What nonsense! Put the phone down or give it to Lucy.'
'Hey, listen! After you left yesterday, I sat with my eyes closed for a long time. I thought that whatever happens after my eyes are closed or whatever I see through my inner consciousness would be a divine vision for me. There, the strangeness of worldly life cannot touch me.

Instead, I can understand the real mystery of life.

Pradyumna went on hearing …..

'At first, a strange darkness surrounded me. I tried to stay still. "I threw away the sense of "self". I tried to bring forth an invisible entity and some bright substance. At that time, a strange sensation was playing within me. I had thought that the positive effects of life would flood my inner being. But alas! No matter how much I tried, violence, hatred, hypocrisy, sarcasm, jealousy, envy, despair, pain, etc. were revealed one by one".

'No matter how hard I tried, I could not eliminate it. I thought my solitude and my unique vision were an excuse. If my transcendental state is a bleak picture of worldly chaos, how mistaken are the people who claim or say they are at peace or will be if they meditate? I am one of them, a fallible human being.'

'I thought, if everything has changed with the changing times, including the scene around me, why should I be indifferent to the world? Rather, I would let my world be as it was earlier. Thinking this, I ran away from there.'

Pradyumna was patiently listening to Mrutyunjay. His feelings were a rush of self-satisfaction in his veins and an oblique excitement in his mind.

Pradyumna said: 'Hey, crazy fellow! Will you burn everything to ashes for self-examination? How can good things come to your mind when injustice and corruption are everywhere, like a shadow? Be aware of yourself for once; you will see that it will never end. Your life and your world will sweeten. If you go through a confusing state again, you will have no more chance to live.'

'Can't you be blessed with the divine eye if you reside in this world?' asked Pradyumna. Mrutyunjay's phone was cut off.

While leaving the hospital, Pradyumna thought Sanjay was narrating Dhrutarastra about the horrors of the Kurukshetra war. Whatever Sanjay was watching was precisely happening: Violence, win and defeat.

During Dhrutarastra's rule, the reflection of Kauravsena's downfall was ardently visible. Suppose you say that Lord Krishna was giving meaningful prophecies to Arjuna. You will know precisely how much hypocrisy is hidden once you see it carefully. Why should you be Sanjay or Dhrutarastra? You are our beloved Mrutyunjay. You cannot conquer death, but you can beat yourself.

After becoming conscious, Pradyumna realized he was saying this to himself and not to Mrutyunjay.

Pradyumna was about to think of something else. At this time suddenly the mobile rang. From the other side, it was heard –'When will you come? The courier has arrived.' Pradyumna replied: 'Open it and see what is there inside. I am on call.'

The wife said: 'It is waxed, and the cover is thick.'

Pradyumna said: 'Yes, open the seal.'

Pradyumna waited for some time.

It was heard again from the other side.

'Yes, it is a thick book. The name of the book is 'Divine

Vision and Divine Consciousness'. On it, there is a photo of Srimandir.'

'Okay, keep it, I'm coming, " said Pradyumna, cutting off the phone.

While returning home, Pradyumna looked at Mrutyunjay's quarters. The door of his house was open! Not only has the door been available, but the heart of Mrutyunjayh has been lit with knowledge of reality. Now, he is back in the real world.

Pradyumna steps a bit faster than earlier. After reaching home, he will look at the book first and read it. After reading it, he will be eagerly waiting to see how much this book transforms him.

Pradyumna steps fast towards his quarters.

The Elephant

When Nitia was a child, he made fun of the elephant. An elephant is a massive animal carrying a considerable body. Its legs are like a tree's trunk, yet it keeps walking and never stops.

Every time the elephant visited the village, Nitia and the other children would gather around it. Nitia's friends danced with delight, marvelling at the long trunk, huge ears, and impressive tusks. They followed the elephant until it gradually vanished on the outskirts of the village.

Nitia strolls beside them, unable to resist the elephant's leisurely pace. He desires the elephant to pick up speed, eager to chase after it. After all, why settle for walking when there's the exhilaration of running? This is precisely why Nitia always makes fun of the elephant.

He sings, "Run, oh elephant, run," instead of saying, "Swing, oh elephant, swing", a phrase he had read in his school book.

Every year, during the harvest season, the elephant arrives. Upon its arrival, Nitia's friends playfully taunt him about his disinterest in the elephant, shouting, "Hey, look, look, the elephant is here!" Nitia would sit with a downcast face but wouldn't react, and over the years, he never developed an affection for the elephant. However, as he grew up, he has come a long way.

"Nitia understands that covering a path doesn't mean merely progressing from one year to another. For him, it implies leading a fulfilling life, earning a livelihood, and managing household affairs. When he mentions a fulfilling life, he emphasizes the importance of hard work and effort, suggesting that one should engage in strenuous labour while physically capable, avoiding laziness. This suggests that Nitia works in a field as a farmer rather than holding a salaried job." He's growing crops and handling his family.

Nitia is too proud of his toughness. However, that evening, as he sipped his evening tea, sentence by sentence, her wife Tulasi burst his toughness and self-obsession like bubbles just by saying just a few words.

Tulasi said something to Nitia, who always stood firm, to help Nitia understand rather than shatter his toughness or self-esteem. She said, "You toil in the fields, cultivating crops with sweat and blood. Isn't that true? However, observe the villagers. Without doing anything, they receive government rice." She continued, "You feel agitated when you hear about the elephant! But, see, a horse is running, and there's also an elephant walking at ease. But both of them are in the same place. In essence, you are the horse, and they are the elephant."

Nitiya's excitement for the elephant also vanished after his wife's words. When he hears such words from his wife, Nitia's eyes never remain fixed in one place. His gaze pierces through the hut's roof, reaching the sky, penetrating the mud walls, and extending to the village road. He remains silent, indicating that Tulasi's words have no influence or power to alter Nitia's mindset.

After that, what Tulasi said was not only about Nitia's

intentions but also a powerful account of worldly life. Tulasi says, 'The government will provide us fifteen kilograms of rice each month. We can sustain ourselves for a few months with the rice we receive yearly. We can sell the surplus grain that would have been used for rice.

Other expenses will also be covered, and you will not have to work so hard to cover the costs of festivals like "Punei Paraba."

Tulsi's talk like this is familiar to Nitia, and Nitia is becoming a statue after hearing this news to Tulasi. But that day, for some reason, Nitiya looked at Tulsi's face without turning his eyes, unlike every other day, as if he wanted to soften his demeanour a little.

Tulasi added a few more words in that hope: "These days, I'm also becoming less proficient in processing the paddy. We wouldn't have to do that if we could get government rice. Just look at my face at least once."

Nitiya looked at Tulasi's face; he didn't just look, he also smiled, as if it was not Nitiya's smile but Tulasi's strength.

Tulasi became more interested in melting Nitiya's toughness. She sat so close to him as if they were newly married.

Nitia was also a little interested in Tulasi's inside and outside points. On this occasion, Tulasi said, "You once said yes to the government rice and saw that many of our problems would be solved."

Tulasi knew that Nitiya would not be angry again today. After ten years of marriage, it wasn't tough for Tulasi to understand when Nitiya got furious when he got upset and when he was happy. So after saying that, she looked at Nitia's face, waiting for what he would say. It seemed to her that this was the last thing… Will the government rice come to the house or not?

Nitiya was probably strengthening himself. That's why he straightened his bent body, shook off the mud-covered rug in his bosom, and threw it over his shoulder. It seemed to Tulasi that he must make a final decision today. Will the government rice come home or not?

"You are right Tulasi," said Nitia. We run our family depending on the crops—our food and drink, festivals, health and everything good and evil. However, no matter how much rice is harvested, it must meet our needs. Besides, the child's education expenses are also necessary. You're right, Tulasi.'

After saying this, Nitia kept looking at Tulasi in such a way that Tulasi understood that only the head of the house knew how difficult it was to run a family. Perhaps he has overcome this hardship. He already understood how vital this government rice is for his family and the world.

Tussi was waiting to hear yes from husband Nitia's mouth. After a while, Nitia said yes, but it was not for government rice. Instead, in arousal of self-confidence and self-esteem. Like, 'Yes, I can.'

Tulasi needed help understanding something. That's why she kept staring blankly at Nitia's face. Nitia said knowingly, 'Are you looking so surprised? I can afford to run my family. Not for good but not for bad. I can feed everyone's stomachs, provide clothes and give them whatever they need when they want.'

A voice came out of Nitia's mouth. 'Why don't you trust me?'

How can she have trust?' Tulasi's mouth was full of

these words. But she couldn't tell. Instead, what came out of her mouth was, 'Yes, I trust you.'

Tulasi's words boosted his confidence and reinforced his self-reliance. He touched Tulasi's shoulder and declared, 'I've decided to acquire and cultivate additional land. Our needs remain unmet due to limited land. This issue won't persist with increased crop production. Just observe. Notice how the villagers have abandoned their fields, leading to unutilized land.'

'No one will say no if I ask them for land', says Nita. 'After all, who else is there so hardworking like me in this village!'

Nitia just stayed there unmoved after saying this. He stood unchanged because he thought he found a new way to live and survive. Tulasi fell silent. Well, she was getting up with many words inside of her mind. Looking at Nitia, she was saying, 'Have I ever doubted your way of taking care of this family!' However, I feel bad that you are working day and night to support this family. It will become more suffocating for you.

Nitia got up and went into the village. Farming begins with the touch of rain at the start of the monsoon. However, he became mentally ready two months before. He not only prepares himself mentally, he also organizes the field. He ploughs the field deeply to let the sun's rays penetrate deeply. And the fields have to be equipped with manure.'

After some time, when Nitia returned home, Tulasi saw that smug look on his face. Suddenly, Tulasi did not understand the reason.

Leaning on the wall and sitting down, Nitia said, 'I went to Bhagirathi Samal's house. As I asked for land, the older man became delighted. He said, "These are the ones who are wandering around." Who cares about the farm? The land has been lying fallow for years. Take it and cultivate it. We will give you whatever you want.' Nitia repeated the last words, saying, 'The old man says, we will give you whatever you want? This is what he says while scolding his child. So, why should we make such a mistake? We'll give him what he deserves.'

Tulasi didn't say anything. She was only looking at Nitia in an empty rhythm. She thought, she married him, made a world with him, how stubborn is he? Well, this man is made of bones, flesh and blood. How much can he work? He'll also break one day? He'll suffocate if he brings more land.

It will be humpy that! That's why he can't believe it. However, seeing her determination to run the family, Tulsi's mind was getting numb. That's why tears came out of her eyes. He took care of himself.

After fetching the land from Bhagirathi Samal, it didn't feel under her feet. After wandering in the hot sun that day, her body was sweating. His face was black, too. However, Tulsi's eyes looked heavy on his face.

After giving rice water to the buffalo, sitting on the stool, and drinking lots of water, his bright face looked even more like the sun.

Tulsi brought the beads from inside the house and asked, 'Even after turning the plough in the field in the summer heat, you have a smile on your face? What kind of man are you?'

Nitia was smiling, but there was no sound. Tulsi's laughter now, when she heard this, is very open. Words came out of it, too. "We know why I was smiling," said Nitia, 'Bhagirathi buddha has given me a piece of good fertile land—heavy phosphate soil. For three years, there has been no ploughing in the field. But today, my plough is the land. '

'If I had a piece of land like this!' saying this, Nitya stopped and suddenly became depressed. Tulsi knew where her grief was. Without thinking any more, he said, 'The shower has come and sat down to roll. Go, take a bath and come. '

Many things are understood even if you don't say it. Nitia regrets that she always needs more land. The zamindari is the property that his father's grandfather built. Whether something else is done or not sold, it remains as constant as it is. Does Nitia have anything wrong with buying a piece of land alone? That's why he always makes up his mind. He often says, 'He who has ears does not have gold... One who has gold has no ears. '

He ploughed the green land, fertilized it and arranged it. Every rainy day, farming is like a war for him. Search for weapons to fight the battle. I was looking for such fertile land for cultivation.

But that year, nature had begun to wreak havoc. The raja was over, the month of Ashadha came and sat down to be half-an-half... However, there was no rain.

Every day, Nitia goes near the fields. He sits on the hill and rolls his hand over the land. He feels like he is moving his hand lovingly over the little one's head. Also, has this soil been shaved on the plough? Is that all right? Even if humans and human beings are different, everyone is tied to each other in the thread of the relationship. So is the soil. No matter how many goons you do, if you lie like that for a few days, it will become one again. Nitia looks up at the sky when he sits like this. But there is no trace of clouds in the sky's chest. On the contrary, even more frightening is the sun.

After that, Nitya reached home with a broken heart. Tussi held out the glass of water. She doesn't know if Nitia, who came in the scorching sun, was satisfied. This has become a routine affair. And Tulsi, too.

That day, after Nitya had finished drinking the water, Tulsi said, "It doesn't rain. But the villagers have no worries or concerns. Government rice is available. That's why when it rains, how much doesn't it rain, how much does it go to them?

What Tulsi wants to say still needs to be understood. He knows, telling everything, Tulsi finally stops by the government rice.

There was a thought in my mind. But, pushing back that thought, Nitia said, 'Why did we always say that we are government rice, government rice? 'Who can this government towel eat stomachs daily?' he added, 'Hold on, it hasn't rained this year. It will be next year. Can't we survive on the paddy you are worried about in our house?"

Tulsi couldn't say anything else. Her soul is always as dull in front of Nitia's tightness. He then went inside the house. She knows that her husband has so much faith in herself that she is the one to lose under no circumstances. The village people will take government rice but not bring it! Thinking of this, Tulsi used to ring every moment.

When the seven-year-old boy coughed while he was sleeping at night, Nitia and Tulsi fell into a tizzy. The boy was getting frustrated. As the night progressed, the coughing subsided. But I had an intense fever when I saw it in the morning.

Nitiya, Tutsi rushed to the hospital with their son. When the doctor said that it was not a common fever, the soil fell from under the feet of both of them. The son is infected with dengue fever. Life-threatening if not appropriately treated. There are better times to think or understand how fever happens and how long it will take to cure. Instead, proper treatment is now essential.

Tutsi asked, now, how do we get the money from? Nitiya said, 'You stay with our son'. I'm going home, and I'm going to harvest the grain that I have; I think the medical expenses will go up.' Saying this, Nitiya was startled by herself. Looking at Tussi's face, it seemed she was also thinking about something.

The money that was harvested has been used, and to be honest, my son is better. They are happy
  after observing the son's face.

'What should we do now?' Tulsi wondered, sitting there dazed that evening. It's not raining. Whether or not farming can be done correctly this year is only possible with certainty. The grain in the house had vanished from the barn as well. What should I eat right now?

When he sat down, Nitia was thinking precisely the same thing. Still, he had no option. Indeed, there are choices. Government-run rice mills. However, he wanted to avoid breaking a long-standing resolution by accepting it. Tussi wanted to say just that, but the words would have come later.

Merely sitting around, Nitia had grown lazy. That night, thoughts about the upcoming year kept him awake. He had only a light nap just before dawn. However, the village boy's voice disrupted his sleep, revealing the arrival of an elephant in the village.

Nitia discarded his resentment toward the elephant, like shedding a blanket from his body. He eagerly wanted to meet the elephant, pondering, 'What's the difference between him and the elephant today?' The elephant is lazy due to its massive body, and he is sluggish because of his circumstances.

This time, Nitia stepped out of the house to see the elephant. He observed children pulling the elephant's tail, throwing stones, and prodding it with sticks. Yet, the elephant continued to move at a slow pace.

As he sat there, Nitia entertained the thought of playfully teasing and scolding the elephant if it were to transform into a human.

At that moment, Tulasi approached with a cup of red tea. Dismissing Nitia's aloofness, Tulasi remarked, 'You mentioned going to the head of the village's home early this morning. Aren't you going? You had to provide our family's name for the ration card.'

'Did I say that?' Nitia responded, surprised. Tulasi turned slightly and clarified, 'You didn't explicitly say that; it was more of a dream. You mentioned this in your sleep. You said you'd go to the Sarpanch (head of the village) and tell him to include our family in the ration list. You also said, "I voted for him; he'll listen to me."'

As usual, Nitiya kept looking shocked at Tulasi. Pulling back Nitiya's wonder veil, Tulasi said again, 'What comes in a dream is only a matter of the mind.'

Nitiya was about to say something, but a group of boys suddenly rose, shouting. When he turned around, a young boy brought a fire stick and rattled the elephant's tail. Suddenly, whatever happened, the elephant startled and started running. The elephant ran so fast that the children couldn't reach him.

Nitiya felt like he was becoming a child again. He got up and ran after the elephant. Then, the elephant ran along the road leading from the village head. Behind the elephant, Nitiya was also running. The elephant was running so fast that Nitiya also couldn't reach him. Nitiya got tired.

In a short time, the elephant disappeared into the distance. Nitiya just stood there. The children who were having fun following the elephant also reached him. They were all searching for the elephant. Nitiya thought to himself, the elephant is such a surprising animal. At first, it went slowly; then it ran so fast that no one could stop it!

Next, Nitiya suddenly started running, surprising all the children gathered there. He came running like that and reached home. When he came out with a spade, Tulasi asked, 'Where are you going? Don't you know that there are cracks in the field due to the lack of rain!'

Nitiya said, 'I'm going to bring the canal water by making a way with this spade to our field.' 'Ah! What can you do?' By that time, Nitiya had gone two steps further. He stood there and said, 'Didn't you see how the elephant ran?'

Tulasi sat down and thought, 'This man would do anything he could, but he'll never bring the government rice home' and cried. Two tear drops fell from her eyes as if they were not teardrops but water flowing into their field.

LAST STORY FOR
MY FATHER

'Why have you shaved your head?' Though the question stirred my heart with emotions, I tried to control myself. I replied with a mild tone, 'My father left for the heavenly abode a few days back.'

The gentleman said, 'Alas!' I am so sorry to ask you this question. He could read my state of mind rightly. Don't think of me otherwise. Inadvertently, I hurt you.

I said, 'Why should I take it otherwise?' Anybody, instead of you, would have asked me the same question! One could have asked me why I had shaved my head!!

That was the last query from the gentleman. Before that, he had understood everything. Where I have been working… whether I have been married or not…I will stay alone or not…he had the answers for all these.

When the house rent was final, I gave the owner an advance amount for two months. My rented house was confirmed.

Finally, the gentleman wanted to know when I would come to stay at his house. I reverted, but eight more days have yet to be completed for the current month. I will stay here on the first date of the coming month. That's Sunday. It will be good for me.

Then I returned home.

It was almost evening. When I entered the room and unlocked the door, darkness spread everywhere. A statue stood there like a shadow. Is it my father? I knew that it was an illusion. After my father's death, I had perceived his image in the void many times. I have realized his lifeless image or shadow. I have also felt the same way on this day. But I had no fear. I knew I wouldn't fear that if he were visible to me in incorporeal form or if his spirit wandered into the surroundings. The reason is straightforward: A father is always a father. He will behave as he used to be with me earlier, even in the other world. He won't do any harm to me.

I was not afraid today. When I switched on, the light dispelled the darkness in the room. I looked around. His memory was stored everywhere. That's the cot where he used to sleep. He used to swing in the plastic armchair in the middle of the room. That chair was carrying my father's load or weight. The cot and the chair are waiting for.

I brought my father to me the moment I realized that his health condition was worsening day by day. I preserved the drawing room of my rented house entirely for him. The room was tiny but dear to me and my favourite. I used to read and write there and enjoy the outside world through the window in my solitude.

I forgot my loneliness while my father was with me. I was busy taking him to the medical to engage myself in various tests of his body, to give him medicines timely and to look after his body. I couldn't realize the time.

At last, time wins over the race of life. Day by day, my father's health weakened. He went into the COMA stage. Then, he left the mundane world forever.

Though he passed away, his movement was apparent every moment in this room. I reached here four to five days back after completing his last rituals at my village. I felt his presence in the air of this room as if the chair and cot installed here were remembering him. I was also mourning silently for him. When I was sleeping in the other room, I used to hear his groan suddenly. I feel like my father is here now. In this room, I had insurmountable pain in my body.

Finally, I decided to change my room. I can't bear the experiences stored in my heart for my father. My family members and friends also consulted me on this matter.

On the first day of the month, I came to my newly rented house with my luggage. One can't tell this a two-storey building entirely. Only one room is on the roof of the building. That room houses a bathroom and a kitchen. The landlord and his wife stay on the ground floor.

After I reached there, the gentleman and his wife welcomed me from the road. Both of them seemed to be happy. The reason for their happiness is not the house rent. One can guess something else.

At this time, the gentleman whom I can call 'Uncle' said, "You won't face any difficulty here. We have a son only. He stays in the U.S.A. He has not come home for the last four years. You are like our son. You can stay here as many days as you want. You will tell us your problems anytime if you encounter them."

The Uncle was about to say something else, but the aunt stopped him, letting him arrange the luggage he had brought in an apple pie order. Let's go down.

Both of them stepped down to the ground floor immediately.

I was tired after decorating everything in the room. I unconsciously slept while flipping over the bed and didn't know how long I slept there.

I woke up from the bed suddenly hearing someone's call "Chinmaya…Chinmaya". The building was on the roadside. I flipped over the bed to find out who was calling. Then I heard the knocks on my door. I was astonished when I heard the name "Chinmaya…Chinmaya" many times from the outside.

From the tone, I guessed he must be the house owner. Again, I thought, if he were 'Uncle', why would he call me "Chinmaya…Chinmaya"? I told my name to him. Has he forgotten my name?

Hearing the knocks on my door again, I suddenly got up from bed. The Uncle entered the room courageously. He was with a teacup. While placing the teacup on the table, he enquired whether I was putting it.

I was shocked to hear the name Chinmaya from his mouth straightaway.

I humbly responded to him, "I am not Chinmaya, Uncle!" I was about to tell him my name then. Avoiding my words, he said, "We, the two, take tea in the evening. Aunt sent me to you to offer a cup of tea to you."

Then I understood that the aunt thought of me as Chinmaya.

Giving a break to my thoughts, he said, 'Please have this cup of tea. Otherwise, it's getting cold.'

Saying so, he left the room. The steam of the tea cup gets dimmed. I realized its hotness while sipping. After taking the tea, I relaxed for a while.

Then I stirred with a question. Why could I not deny it while Uncle was bringing tea for me? Why would I not tell him that I don't take tea? Otherwise, I would have told him why you took pain for me. I was about to go outside; I would have taken a cup of tea there.

"Why couldn't I say?" I feel uncomfortable then and there. Being well-decked, I wandered outside for some time; I was new.

After taking dinner from the hotel, when I reached my room, it was almost 10.00 pm. I walked fast, being aware of time.

While I pressed the calling bell, Uncle and Aunt opened the door. The Uncle asked, "Did you go to your friend's house, Chinmaya?"

Again, I was shocked by Chinmaya's call. But, I couldn't muster my courage to rebel against this call as it hinted at proximity.

The aunt said while smiling, we were going to bed. We were reminded suddenly that you didn't come back. We were waiting for you. The Uncle said, breaking his silence after a while, "Don't worry, Chinmaya! You can return at your convenience. But you will press the calling once you reach the door. I will get up from my bed to open the door."

After talking to me, they went to bed. I stepped up the staircase to my room. Moonlight was spread on the roof. I stared at the sky wholeheartedly. The cloudless sky seemed to be clear and bright. The stars were marked dim. My father seemed to be somewhere in the stellar bodies, I thought. He is watching me.

I couldn't recognize myself as if I were a stranger, not by the call of an invisible spirit of my father. I was changed within a moment. Someone's gentle call transformed me.

I couldn't look at the sky this time. Then I returned to my

room. I couldn't feel the memories of my father the way they were suspended at my earlier rented house. Though I brought that cot and chair with me after changing my rented house, these were not of my father. I placed them resting on the walls in one corner of the room; I couldn't feel my father's invisible presence on them.

I slept at night. When I woke up in the morning, I felt fresh and energetic. I was hasty to go to my office after my daily routine work. The Uncle reached me, arranging breakfast on a plate. The door was open.

Their love and affection bowled me within a few days. I couldn't get rid of them. Though I was ashamed of it, I couldn't express myself. I was not only unprepared for their presence but I was also bent before them.

The aunt said, "Will it be enough for you, Chinmaya? I was telling your aunt to add two more chapattis to the plate. Your aunt said you don't know the children of this generation. They are so busy with work that they forget to take food. Or else, if they take more, they will gain more weight. They are very conscious of their health."

With Uncle's warnings, I had my breakfast. Immediately, he said you take your food; I am bringing two more chapattis and a bowl of curry.

While swallowing food unmindfully, I coughed. Uncle was worried for me. Offering a glass of water, he gently caressed my back.

I was humiliated. Sometimes, man becomes talkative if he is glued to the thread of love, affection, and proximity. I felt exactly like that. This eloquence made me both unprepared and silent simultaneously.

I humbly expressed, "No, Uncle, It's enough for me."

He didn't tell me anything. Wonderful! He took the plate with me after my breakfast, despite my denial.

An incident after two days! It was a Sunday. It was precisely before a week I stayed here. It was my first holiday. I took a rest in my room. Then I thought I would visit my village that day. When I was on the horns of a dilemma, my Uncle and Aunt warned me not to go anywhere. You will relish lunch with us at noon.

The aunt said, 'Your Uncle is fond of taking mutton. But he takes alone. He doesn't bring mutton as he is the only one to have it.'

Today, he desires non-veg items; you don't deny him, Chinmaya. She told me to be at home.

I was remembering my father's words. My father was fond of taking fish and meat. My Dad can't eat if anybody sits beside him. He puts a piece of fish or meat from his share on my mother's plate. My mom gets irritated. He doesn't listen to her. Today, my Uncle and Aunt share their meat curry with me affectionately. My eyes were full of tears.

I remembered my father intensively. I was hiding my tears cautiously. Though I was taking food, I mourned my Dad silently. I felt them as my parents instead of my Uncle and Aunt. Uncle was sitting before me as my father.

After lunch, my Uncle asked me if I could ask you a favour. I stopped then at the staircase while stepping up. Uncle said it would be Monday tomorrow. Can you help us visit Lord Shiv's Temple? We must offer one hundred and eight *belpatra* (Wood apple leaves) on *Shivalinga*. If you are with us, we will be comfortable. You will extend the *belpatras* to the Brahman's hand. You are like my son. Our family priest said, "If we do this, our sorrows and evils will vanish.

The aunt told me, "There won't be any problem reaching your office." If we go to the temple at 7.00 am, we can return by 9.00 am from there. Before movement, I will prepare our breakfast. We will eat together, and you will go to your office.

I was a little hesitant and said to them, "My father's death is yet to be the first year. Entering the temple is strictly prohibited. As you are saying, I can't deny."

Uncle said, "No mishap will come to you, Chinmaya." Religion is a belief system. If we have faith in God, everything will be set right. No calculation of vice and virtue is made before the belief system. He also opined, "Are we not like your parents, Chinmaya?"

I was surprised to hear this from his mind. I searched for my father, having returned to my home. I stood silently before his photo for an hour. Then I got relaxed.

There was no rush at the temple. Both Uncle and Aunt were prepared with everything. While Uncle was extending *belpatra* to me, the priest asked about *gotra* (lineage). Before I say anything, Uncle told me, "Chinmaya, Nagasya Gotra!"

I was so astonished that the *Belpatra* automatically fell on the *Shivalinga*. My hand was still and unmoved.

I can't realize when the wood apple leaves are showered upon the *Shivalinga*. Then Uncle came to me and said, 'Let's us return our home.'

I always mean 'home' as my own. Home is the place where my father stays. A place encircled by four walls is full of unfathomable love and affection. That space where we share our sorrows and happiness. That's my home. But here, Uncle and Aunt led me into another 'home', stirring my mind with innumerable questions. One question that always haunted me was, 'Has uncle offered *belpatra* on the *Shivalinga* for me?'

I was wavering with this question for many days. That day, suddenly, I discovered. "Uncle can't hide an unknown happiness with him." It comes out spontaneously. In the meantime, I was very close to my Uncle and Aunt. I was not ashamed to ask this. Then Uncle replied, "Yes, I have forgotten to tell you that my son is returning from America today. We were afraid of some days earlier when the Indians there faced issues relating to their jobs because of their VISA. We are fortunate that he got a job here in India now."

I couldn't sleep at night. When I was unaware of the time that night, I heard the noise on the ground floor. Uncle's son may have reached late at night. That's why I listened to the sound last night. Then, I slept freely and comfortably.

It's the early dawn. Then, the uncle called "Chinmaya… Chinmaya". I got up from the bed suddenly and rushed down the staircase.

Having reached there, I saw Uncle and his son talking to each other happily. Uncle noticed me at that time.

I asked, "Did you call me Uncle?"

He said to me, "No! I was calling my son!"

Uncle introduced me to his son, "This is my son, Chinmaya."

I needed clarification for a while about whom Uncle was addressing Chinmaya. It's whether to me or his son.

At this time, Uncle told his son, "He stays on our first floor as a renter."

I was shocked as if someone was hammering my heart. I was also surprised when my Uncle asked me my name before his son.

Uncle said to me, "Don't take it otherwise. I can't remember your name or what you told me that day. I have completely forgotten your name."

After this, the father-son duo looked at me strangely. I felt very awkward there.

I stepped up without saying anything.

I looked at my Dad's photo thirstily and invoked him helplessly.

I waited for him when he would come out of his photo frame and tell me not to remember me. Wherever you may be, you will feel I am always with you. I waited for a while. He couldn't come out of the frame. But, in that photo frame, my Dad was transformed into a live statue for me.

I clasped that photo of my father closely. Then I started crying aloud. I gradually became conscious of my presence.

MOTHER'S FACE

How was Mother's face? Chinmaya thought, 'Is it a question?' or 'else to whom is he asking?' When a man loses his self-confidence, he questions himself. He asks time and again. Has he lost his self-confidence? But he has forgotten his mother's face. He waits for WhatsApp messages. He will see his mother's face.

Mobile's network is extraordinary! Sometimes it works, sometimes not. The distance between the town and the village is only twenty kilometres. Nobody worries about this distance. Within no time, one can reach the village and come back. Sometimes, we feel the village getting transformed into a city within a few years. People think of it only. When the mobile network doesn't function, the village is only a village.

Chinmaya was worried about the phone's network. Who will talk about the internet when there is no network? That's why he often strolls on the roof. He sees his mother's face hazily wherever he roams. He was with his mother from the day he became conscious of the world to the day of his mother's death. But he tries his best to see the clear image of his mother; he fails to get its reflection in the mirror of his mind. For that, he thinks he has lost his self-confidence. Or his mother is not with him, or he is not with the invisible spirit of his mother.

He thought about this and looked at the mobile many times. Chinmaya got irritated not finding the network. He was saying to himself that all others are right! A village is always a village, whatever communication systems are extended there. Chinmaya needs that internet facility only. He knows that he will receive his brother's message after some time. He will ask whether I have seen the model of my mother's face. If I saw, why had I not replied? The WhatsApp message box will be filled up with questions.

He will not rebuke Chinmaya only but the entire village. While scolding, he will forget that he was once born here. He grew up here enjoying the fresh air and water and playing on this land. He will highlight the differences between the town and the village while rebuking the topic. He will behave like others.

Chinmaya has known his brother well from childhood. His elder brother is five years older than him. This age gap has not brought any difference between the two. The difference is his brother's merit. My father's eye was on him as he was the family's elder son. He was also studying well in the class. After getting through the scholarship in class VII, he looked at the Government High School in our closest town. From that day onwards, he has been away forever. After graduating, he joined the Intermediate Science Course at Ravenshaw College, Cuttack. After that, he joined the Indian Institute of Technology, Delhi. He rarely visited our village while studying there. He gets inclined to my mother for the number of days he stays in the town and doesn't come to other's hold. After graduating from I.I.T., he left for America. It has already been ten years since the day he left our village, and he has not returned home. He has been cut off from all kinds of relationships.

When my brother went to America, there were no email, Facebook, or WhatsApp facilities. For a developed country like America, it may be a trifle. But, in our country, these apps were rarely used. And it's better not to ask about the village. At that time, Dad was alive. Dad was waiting for my brother's call like a pied crested cuckoo. He was passing the time waiting for his brother's call.

My father must wait at least twenty hours for the phone call. Sometimes, he will wait for a month. He can't call from this side. If he gets a call by chance, my Dad Dad becomes thrilled. He revolves around the space in happiness before receiving the call like Chinmaya making rounds on the rooftop.

He cleans the phone first with his towel. He extends this hospitality as if he welcomes a guest to our home. He gets overwhelmed by the phone call from his brother.

Chinmaya says, 'Dad, receive the call first.' Otherwise, it will be disconnected. While you clean the phone, some buttons may automatically be pressed, and the call will be disconnected.

He can't listen to me. He can't bear the third person's entry in his conversation with his brother. Though he doesn't say anything, it can be understood from his gesture. My mother also runs fast from somewhere to my father for a conversation with my brother. She is interested in talking to my brother. Sometimes, she cries.

But my Dad left the phone slowly; he told him everything individually. He first enquires about his health and surroundings. Their discourse reveals they are discussing my brother's new position in the scholarship race. Then he spells out, chattering everything one by one.

While talking to my father, my Mom tries to snatch the phone away from him. But my DadDad moves a little. He then says, 'Your Mom is here. She is having multiple health issues. She always suffers from coldness.'

Having heard this, my Mom cries. My DadDad can understand this, 'After I have a word with you, you will talk to your mom.'

But he doesn't leave the phone so early. He knows it won't come again once he disconnects the call. He has to share so many ideas. He should be aware of not only my mother and Chinmaya. He has stored many incidents in the villages, such as someone getting married, someone passing away, etc.

Chinmaya gets afraid of hearing about him when my DadDad tells my brother. He understands that if my brother starts talking about me, he won't stop, and my DadDad will only be a listener. Dad says only, "What else could he do? I had concentrated upon you only. If both of you stayed away from us, how would we, old fellows, manage at home? Rather, it was better for him to stay here for us. At least he can be a teacher at the village school. He will stay at home and look after our properties, and us too. Nowadays, teachers are also receiving good salaries."

My brother must be expressing his disapproval at my father's words. His face colour changes; my DadDad gets caught from his untold gestures toward the mobile. My Dad makes me (Chinmaya) stand last for everything.

Then he gives the mobile phone to my mother. My Mom talks to my brother for a while. Then, the phone gets disconnected.

Now, Dad pours all his anger upon me. He says, 'What do you think? Have I told all the lies to your brother to save you? And I headed all the blemishes. The fact is that I don't want him to get paid for all this staying far away from us. Only for that, I have said so.'

Dad makes me hear many points, 'How many times has your brother told you to study well and get appointed to good jobs? Hasn't he told you? Are you listening to him?'

While saying so, Dad expresses his unhappiness with abusing him. Chinmaya angrily says, "I don't think of him; why he thinks of me?"

Then my DadDad becomes impatient. Calling my mother, he says, 'Listen to what he says. He should at least think that his brother is worried about this family staying at a distant place. He is thinking about him. But he is blaming his brother.'

It happens not only once or twice but many times. It happens whenever my brother rings up. I understand how far my father loves my brother.

Now, my Dad is no more. After his death, out of grief, my mother also passed away.

When my father died, how he was restless to see my brother at least once. He had pride and honour for my brother in the ten villages, but that shattered. He was talking nonsense. I could have stopped him from going to America! I could have told them he did not need to work at a faraway place. You can get an excellent job in our country based on your education. My father tried to prove that his elder son was second to none then. He was so excited that he could not think of it then. Dad was saying all this indistinctly at his deathbed.

My father's death message couldn't reach my brother. When he rang up to us, he knew that. By that time, all funeral rites were over. Having heard my father's death, he couldn't bear it and started crying, holding the phone. Then he cut off the phone call but didn't tell me whether he would come home.

My Mom was restless. She asked me repeatedly, "Did you tell your brother to come to our home? He has been away from us for many years. Mourning him, his father died. Will he come to see me after my death? If he calls you next time, you will tell him to come home at any cost."

After that, his brother called him many times.

That day, he rang up and told me, "He had a crux with a girl in Delhi while studying. That girl is also working in a company in the U.S.A. He is getting married to that girl shortly." He also opined, "He is staying so far that even Chinmaya and Mom can't reach them easily. Moreover, at the time of marriage, there will be neither a reception nor an altar for chanting any mantras. In the presence of some friends, a paper of contract will be signed by both of us. That's all."

My Mom heard this. She cried, 'Why is he saying so?' Has he married in any other religion? We may not go. I am sceptical about whether there will be chanting of mantras on the altar. That is our ritual and tradition. How can I be debarred from that? What will his father think about staying in the heavenly abode?

Chinmaya said, "Mom! What epoch are you in? Is my brother within your reach or caught by you? He must have forgotten your tradition, altar for marriage, and chanting of mantras on the altar at the time of marriage."

After hearing Chinmaya, my Mom started crying. While

crying, she said, 'He got highly educated. Is it his knowledge and wisdom? He seems to be irreligious.'

Chinmaya thought of himself as a culprit.

He soliloquizes, "She could have supported my brother. He is staying in America. He is earning a lot. Considering his position or post, he has chosen his life partner! She didn't say that he brought unnecessary pain to my Mom's mind."

My Mom couldn't keep her anger on my brother for long. She is so delighted for my brother. There was a reason behind this. After a few months, my brother suddenly rang up, "O Chinu! You will erect a father's statue at the homestead land we have at the roadside after constructing a porch and making a roof. No rainfall or sunlight can touch my father's statue." He also said, "You will raise a boundary around our homestead land so that no cows can cross that boundary to enter the land. He is ready to spend money for this."

Having heard my brother, my mother cried a lot. Her tears were of sorrow and happiness. She was reminded of my father. Memories of my father reverberated within her heart. For that, she was crying. Again, my brother's words about the installation of my father's statue brought tears to her eyes.

Chinmaya never discards his brother's words out of fear or love. My parents and the entire village are proud of my brother. However, his village is in a hinterland. Rivers surround it. It is inaccessible from every angle. Everybody is hesitant to work here at first sight. When people in this place struggle for their lives at every nook and corner, who will ask about their studies here? Is being employed in the U.S.A. out of this critical place difficult? My father was most respected in the village for that. He feels pride for my brother. I also earn respect for my brother in the locality. I never let down my brother's word.

My father seemed to appear in another form. When we saw that statue, my father had returned to us again. He had been with them to revive and reassume in their lifeless flow of life. The statue is a lively and exact replica of my father, and everybody praises it.

My brother was anxious to see my Dad's statue. After that, he asked about that statue whenever he talked to me over the phone.

My brother says, "Hey, I am overwhelmed to glance over my Dad's statue! That's not the statue but a live image. At any cost, you send me a photo of that."

He also said, "When I left for America, I couldn't bring any photo of my father or mother. I have thought repeatedly to hang my parents' photos in the drawing room. I will feel their presence every moment. But, I was so stupid to bring their photos with me while departing my home."

He said so and instructed me how to send the photos to him. But Chinmaya could not understand that. Since that day, an image of my father's statue could not reach him.

After that, he never reminded me of that while calling me over the phone.

After my Dad's demise, my Mom also passed away. My Mom was bedridden for some days before she left for the heavenly abode. She was agitated to see my brother on her deathbed when my brother rang me up over the phone. Then my brother said, "I can't come home because they have been recently blessed with a son."

After my parents' death, my brother rarely rings me up. Though he distanced himself from me over time, in every telephonic conversation, he said I was unfortunate to stay away from home for years. I couldn't see any one of my parents before their death.

He was saying so, but before the villagers, his image and persona gradually weakened. They severely ridiculed him for not joining the last rites of his parents.

Chinmaya was lonely after his parents died. His brother didn't visit him at least once. He often thought his brother would come to console him in his loneliness and ask him how he had led his life. These two brothers can be together to reminisce about their past life and parents' absence.

But we want things to happen differently. In the meantime, many years pass by, not only in the calendar but in every field. Topography, communication facilities and the lifestyle of the villagers changed. Everybody in the village has a smartphone, though there is a network problem. Time has changed. People also change themselves with time.

Chinmaya has also bought a smartphone after his brother's warning. He did so forcefully and with many hesitations. His brother asked him whether you needed more money or time to purchase from the market. Without any further delay, he bought the smartphone. Then he understood why his brother repeatedly asked him for the phone that day.

He instructed me to send him a photo of our father's statue soon.

Chinmaya was shocked.

He remembered seeing the image of our father's statue. Chinmaya knew that and was surprised.

He became aware of the astonishment and irritation. Why are you looking at me so strangely? At that time, you needed help sending it. Now, you can send through WhatsApp comfortably. Try to send the image today at any cost.

His brother's instruction made Chinmaya's veins and arteries alert. After his mother's death, he has not paid any attention to his father's statue, even cleansing the statue. He had never expressed or mapped his sorrows and happiness before the statue. He was spending his time alone after all had departed. He was entirely unmindful of that.

His friend Saubhagya often told him, "Go sit and express freely and frankly before the statue. Your father will listen to you certainly. You will be relaxed."

After his parents deserted him, he had been possessed of self-respect and touchy. Since that day, he has not visited that statue.

There is no way to escape. I have told you before that wherever Chinmaya may be, the fear of his brother frequently haunts him. The first reason for his fear was the warning for studies. Though he is grown up, the same fear still haunts him. The second reason is his brother's education, personality and capability to retain the family's social prestige. If all these are added, his brother always stands up before him anew and uniquely. How can he disobey his brother's word today?

Chinmaya took one day to wash the statue before taking a snapshot. He bought a white shawl for the statue and garlanded it, purchasing fresh flowers from the market. He burned a bunch of incense sticks in the front. He shot a photo of the statue and sent the same to his brother.

Then he awaited his brother's reply. One day passed, but no response reached him, nor did he make any phone calls or send messages through WhatsApp. Chinmaya was worried. He soliloquized, "Has my brother not seen the photo?"

Saubhagya said, "You can check whether the blue coloured marks are below the photos sent. If so, he has seen. Maybe he has not responded to you because of his busy schedule."

Chinmaya could not free himself from his apprehension. An unknown fear engulfed him. He knows his brother from his childhood. He gets irritated if there is a slight deviation in anything. His disciplined life and concentration have placed him high in society. He is awaiting the exam result, not for his brother's answer. Chenmaya felt so.

I received the message early in the morning and thought I was unaware of the time in America. I found a message in the WhatsApp alert condition.

Unwrapping the bed sheet from the face, Chinmaya was reading the message. Initially, it was blurred. The message becomes legible. He rebuked him in the message. He perspired seeing the message.

He wrote in the message, "Is this the statue of our father? Is he with this type of face? Have you installed our father's statue or sent me somebody else's statue? Haven't you cheated me? Don't think about staying at a distance. I have forgotten my father, and you will hoodwink me easily."

He also wrote, "Our Dad and Mom's statue will be placed side by side. Their installation will be so that no one will say they are made for each other. Yes, listen to me! I will send you the design of the statue from here through WhatsApp. Showing the sculptor, you will erect the statue. See! You won't deceive me. If I ever visit our village, I will go to the place where my parents are adorned as statues."

Chinmaya can't concentrate after receiving his brother's message. He is strolling on the roof. There is no mobile network. In the meantime, he remembers his father and mother spontaneously. He is disturbed. He was worried and tilted about his father's statue in loneliness.

Chinmaya asked himself where the fault lies. The most renowned sculptor of the city inscribed the statue. I reached the sculptor with the photo of my father taken a few days before my father's death. Nobody can believe such a lively statue of my father to be built. The villagers and my mother, who knows my father well, have commended the statue as lively: the same forehead, nose, and eyes. Father stands up here. Still, my brother says that the statue needs to be better-formed!

At this time, Saubhagya called me from his home's front. Chinmaya was stepping down the staircase; he couldn't remove his parents from his mind.

Having heard all this, Saubhagya said, "Why are you so worried? You will see the image of your mother your brother will send you. You will compare and contrast and mark the difference. Based on that, you will build the statue."

"But I haven't received the message yet."

"O, this is a village, not the town! There must be a network problem. Once connected, it will function. You are so worried that your brother is standing before you and scolding you."

"You can't understand this! Now I cannot understand one point: my brother says he doesn't have the photos of our parents. Then, how will he design our mother's face?"

By that time, Chinmaya had already kicked off his bike. He couldn't hear Chinmaya's words. He left saying, 'See you soon.'

He was stirred by the question he was asking Saubhagya.

Then he ran to his father's statue. He observed it minutely.

He felt his presence deeply. He seems to be overwhelmed finding his father in proximity.

Chinmaya questions, looking at his father's statue, "Dad! Can you tell me whether this is your statute or not? Have I made any mistake in recognizing you or building your statue?"

Dad seems petrified by a lifeless object hidden somewhere in the statue installed. His brilliance of masculinity is reproduced in a stone. Chinmaya knew "His Dad wouldn't listen to him, the way he didn't pay any heed to him in his childhood. Now, he is not with him. This is not his only anguish, but he is crying in distress, not finding his father as lively now."

Chinmaya knows that it is not easy to be relieved from its clutch. One searches for shelter after losing self-confidence. Chinmaya was seeking that. He had faith in the villagers this time. He called some villagers to opine on the statue raised. Among them was Uncle Pramod, who had seen his father since childhood. He also said, "Ah, the replica of Nakula!" while embracing my Dad's Dad's statue, Chinmaya's eyes were full of tears. His brother had not only questioned him about the structure of the statue but doubted his feelings reserved for his father.

Chinmaya returned from his father's statue. It was mid-day. He needed to take food on time. He was disturbed. He could not realize the hunger. As he is tied by his parents' memory this day, he has forgotten his thirst and hunger.

He sees not only his father but also his mother's face. If he searches for his mother's photo at home, he won't get it. His Mom was so beautiful that one could forever store her image in one's heart and mind. While my DadDad was with her, she was looking like a goddess. The entire village says this. She never unveils her wrapper from her head. The wrapper enhances her beauty and solemnity. After his father's death, she has been completely changed. In her face, there was neither any smile nor any lustre. She has lost her brilliance in loneliness.

When he remembers his mother's face, he finds hers dry and indifferent.

Sitting on the public pavilion, he checked the mobile network. Is there any new message? It took time for him to receive the message. He was more disturbed by the mother's face. He was confused for his mother's face. How can she be? What was his mother's natural face? What has he seen? Or what design of his mother's face has his brother sent to him through WhatsApp message?

Chinmaya had slept early thinking about this. While sleeping, he was troubled by this conflict. His brother said, 'The photo he sent him is not his father's.' That's why his brother will send him a design of their mother's image that his brother has remembered.

Saubhagya was right to say that having seen the image of his mother sent by his brother; he would be able to know where the fault lies in his father's statue. Otherwise, his brother will deceive him by raising unnecessary conflicts in his mind.

Chinmaya checks his mobile repeatedly until he sleeps. But he has yet to receive a message. In the dream, he saw his mother's face.

He got up from the bed with the alert call of the message. His brother sent him a message. The design of his mother's face was inside the message box.

Chinmaya's eyes were wonder-struck at his mother's photo. He said, "It was my mother's face ten years back! Then, is my brother searching for my father's ten years earlier image? That time when he had seen his father for the last time."

Now Chinmaya understood why his brother was angry with him—my mother's image he had accurately designed says of the image of ten years back. Until now, my brother has stored those images of my Dad and Mom in his heart and mind! Chinmaya could not believe this.

Gone are those ten years. Time has changed. Time has also influenced my parents' physique. By the time they passed away, my parents were with different physiques. There was a vast difference between the images of their deathbeds and those designed by his brother ten years back.

But his brother's imagination had imagined his mother's image ten years back. It is very tough for someone to reproduce an imaginative figure into a real one. He has misunderstood his brother unnecessarily.

Chinmaya has determined to build and install his mother's statue. He will reinstall a new statue of his father along with his mother. Those statues will be built as conceived in his brother's mind. Otherwise, one can mark the age differences between them.

THE ARTISAN

After hearing this, Chinmaya Babu was surprised. Thinking of what to say, his hand clutching the phone bent downward slowly. Yet, the 'hello...hello' came out of the telephone in whispers. 'No, we haven't?' He hung up after saying this.

Nowadays, Chinmaya Babu can't hear anything properly, so he has increased the phone volume. However, his wife, Gitanjali, can't bear this high volume. Despite knowing her health condition, Chinmaya Babu roared, 'Let me hear what you say.'

Gitanjali then walked from the room she was in towards the open space where Chinmaya Babu was sitting and said, "How many times have I asked you to lower the volume? " You know I have chest pain, yet you pay no heed to my illness."

Gitanjali breathed heavily as she got up. She grabbed the nearest chair and sat down.

When the phone rang again, Chinmaya Babu was about to say a few words. But, he did not pick up the call until he had spoken with his wife, and there, his wife was in pain as long as the phone was ringing. He got anxious instead and asked his wife, "pick it up....pick it up". Chinmaya Babu was a tough nut; he retorted, "You know pretty well that I, too, am unwell. My ears cannot properly hear, nor can't my eyes properly see!"

Gitanjali stayed silent. Helplessly, as she gazed at Mister Chinmaya, she saw that he had already picked up his phone. The person on the other side spoke again, "Sir, I am contacting you from the Jagannath Mandir regarding the order of the meals you had placed. The order is ready. We have prepared the order of a hundred meals you had already paid in advance. It's time for lunch, and your guests must also be waiting. Even after that, you are maintaining silence."

Chinmaya Babu could partially hear whatever was spoken to him. He silently cut the call When he realized Someone had called him mistakenly. He then pondered how the trivial matter, because of this minor miscommunication, may bring a lot of worries and complications to both parties. He later wondered why he was worrying about them. They would eventually contact and sort it out themselves. He then sat in a steady composure without paying any attention to the phone anymore.

Gitanjali broke his composure and asked him, "Who had called you? You seem to be worried."

"Why would I be worried...?" the words which came out of the phone rang in his ears once again while he was saying this. He couldn't keep things to himself anymore and told his wife, "Someone from some temple had called me to inform me about the order of meals I had previously placed. The food was ready, and he asked me to pick it up. O, for whom is this food? Who am I? Why should I get it picked?"

There was silence for a while. Gitanjali wondered what to say next, as she couldn't say anything. Chinmaya Babu suffered from this silence. He yawned loudly, sat down while resting his back towards the wall, and said out of the blue:

"Do you remember we planned to follow the rituals of the Shohala Puja (at age sixteen, the ceremonies parents celebrate for their children) and feed the needy? "

Chinmaya Babu straightened his bare body as he sat down and took off his glasses to look at Gitanjali with wide eyes. Gitanjali, with a heavy heart, spoke. " Is this to be forgotten that I'd forget? Then, why are you recalling it? We have left many things behind and forgotten them as well. I have faked to have forgotten I left whatever memory behind. Then why are you bringing it up again?"

Gitanjali maintained a stoic silence, but Chinmaya Babu couldn't sit calmly. He spoke again, "Do you recall why we pledged to perform this ritual? Do you remember?"

"Why do you dredge up the past today? Have you no sympathy for me? I've often told you that revisiting old memories shatters only my heart. It has taken a toll on my health. Do you want me to perish?"

Gitanjali's words left Chinmaya Babu speechless. Just then, the phone rang, but in his agitation, he couldn't locate it amid the tangled bedsheets. Despite the chaos, Chinmaya Babu remained composed, confident that the caller wasn't from the temple. "I've confirmed twice that I'm not the one they seek. If they're rational, they won't question me again," he muttered.

Gitanjali, impatient, shouted, "Will you answer the phone, or should I go to the other room?" Calmly, Chinmaya Babu replied, "I'm trying to find it; I don't know where it's ringing from."

Gitanjali could understand his helplessness. She suppressed her pain and suggested, "It must be from the temple."

Finally locating the phone, Chinmaya Babu mused, "Are they intoxicated? Why will they call me again?

"Well, respond to it now …" Gitanjali said, blocking her ears.

Chinmaya Babu got disturbed after the call ended. The stress was evident on his face.

He removed Gitanjali's hands from her ears, pleading, "Will you attend the call? Or will you stand still?"

Out of curiosity, Gitanjali asked, "Who called this time? You used to worry about not receiving any calls before. Today, you're getting multiple calls. Shouldn't you be happy? Then why are you depressed now?"

Chinmaya Babu replied somberly, "You've forgotten, Gitanjali. We received this phone hoping for a call from our son. And now, the matter is beyond our reach. Why should I be happy?" With worry etched on his face, he neared his bed.

"What happened? Why the long face?" Gitanjali asked, surprised.

"Gita, that person from the temple is obstinate. He claims I placed the order. He confirmed the name on the receipt as Mr Chinmaya Mahapatra. How can I deny it now?"

Chinmaya explained his frustration. Understanding his predicament, Gitanjali tried to soothe him, saying, "We didn't place the order. Let them say what they want; it's not our concern. Let them say what they want; why don't you remain silent?"

"They've warned us to be home, or else we'll have to pay for their transportation once they send us the food," Chinmaya said hurriedly, with a tone of desperation. Looking at Gitanjali, he asked, "What should we do now?"

Gitanjali, though her chest trembled, remained composed.

"Do they know our address? Let's see how they send it."

Chinmaya Babu stressed, "Our address is on the receipt. They'll transport the same through a vehicle. How long will it take to reach us?" Chinmaya Babu was terrified, and his forehead beaded with sweat.

Bewildered, Chinmaya Babu sat down.

Trying to reassure him, Gitanjali said, "Don't worry. We have not prepared our lunch yet. If the food from the temple reaches our home, we won't have to cook. We can share it with our neighbours. The surplus amount will go to the dump yard."

"How can you think of throwing God's offerings? It's a sin," Chinmaya fretted.

Gitanjali, at a loss for words, couldn't say anything. The pain in her chest had escalated. But she suppressed it and didn't let it show.

Chinmaya Babu suggested, "What if we distribute the prasad in the nearby settlement? Some may be hungry, while others must be starving. They must be rolling like that in the dust. We have no power, do we? Instantly, he came up with an idea, "Wouldn't it be possible if we called them here instead?"

He continued, "Remember, Gita, those hundred people we were supposed to feed for our son's favour? They must have been children, maybe a bit younger than him. We proposed that, right?"

Avoiding any mention of her son, Gitanjali pretended not to hear. "What if the food doesn't reach us? We'll be in trouble. It will be like going from frying pan to fire." she expressed concern.

Chinmaya Babu sighed, saying, "Yes…. you're right.

What else can we do right now? We have to wait silently."

After a while, he suggested to Gitanjali, "Go and rest. I am also lying down on this bed for a while."

Truly Chinmaya Babu lay down. Gitanjali, dragging her weary body, moved across the room. Yet, much lingered unsaid, like the passing day or the fading night, a multitude of thoughts left unspoken. Chinmaya Babu might have wanted to say something, and Gitanjali would have added to it. The culmination of this conversation would have embodied their son.

The thought of their son never left their minds. They were absorbed in thoughts and unable to express anything. If ever they reached the mouth, they got stuck or lost.

Pretending to sleep, both Chinmaya Babu and Gitanjali couldn't sleep. Hunger grew with time. Gitanjali couldn't stay still and reached the room where Chinmaya Babu rested.

Chinmaya Babu put his hand on his forehead. His closed eyes now opened in worry, tears that were about to flow dried off unnoticed. Gitanjali sensed his tears.

"Were you crying?" she asked. Startled, Chinmaya Babu denied, "No, I'm not."Gitanjali persisted, "How long will you pretend? You're crying, and so was I. Yet, these tears stay within us. How long can we avoid it?"

Chinmaya Babu was silent; how come the talkative person sat mute now? Gitanjali understood his plight but thought shedding tears could have relieved Chinmaya Babu."

"Our tears turned into ice, didn't they?" As the fading light from the window indicated the approaching sunset, Chinmaya Babu remarked. During lunch hour, they passed unnoticed, their hunger forgotten.

Realizing the time, Gitanjali exclaimed, "No one has

come yet!" Both Gitanjali and Chinmaya Babu were hungry.

Walking towards the clock on the wall, Chinmaya Babu heard the phone sound, but the screen stayed dark. Time ticking away, he was clueless.

Feeling her husband's helplessness, Gitanjali declared loudly, "It's around 4 o'clock, I guess."

Returning to bed, Chinmaya Babu acknowledged, "Yes, it's already 4 o'clock. When will we eat? Is Someone playing tricks on us again to cause trouble?"

Unable to answer, Gitanjali felt the increasing pangs of hunger. Her eyes welled up as she suggested, "It's already late. Who else will come? Let's have some flattened or puffed rice. Or... should I cook something?"Chinmaya Babu responded, "When will you cook, and when will we eat? Bring over here the flattened or puffed rice."

While eating, the phone rang again, causing distress to Chinmaya Babu, who was contemplating whether to answer.

Worried, Gitanjali urged, "If it's the same number, don't answer."

"My eyesight is not good; I can't see whose number it is," Chinmaya Babu replied and then picked up the call.

"To my surprise, it is from the temple", leaving him impatient. Though he didn't wish to hear anything, he was too tired to remove the phone and cut the call.

"Was the food good? You were late in taking away the food. Or else, you must have relished piping hot food". Chinmaya Babu, having nothing to answer to this, remained silent. The other side replied: "Please don't mind us calling you this frequently. We must ensure the satisfaction of our respective customers. Hence, please let us know, was the food okay?" Chinmaya Babu's silence compelled the other person to say, "Fine. Do not answer. Your silence has provided our answer. We won't disturb you again anymore this was our last call."

Chinmaya Babu heard the assurance that they wouldn't call again. By then, Gitanjali had stopped eating. She was so hungry a while back. She was eating as if it were her last day. Yet, the contemplation of her mind had satisfied her hunger.

Chinmaya Babu asked: "Why did you stop eating? Please eat."

Inquiring, she asked, "Who called this time?"

"It was from the temple. Be assured that we won't get calls from the temple anymore. So, continue your food. And serve me something as well. I'm hungry!" Chinmaya Babu said in one breath and later dived into his food.

Without further questions, Gitanjali brought over the remaining mashed flattened rice. As they ate, Chinmaya Babu revealed, "They were asking if the prasad were okay."

Chinmaya Babu laughed first. Gitanjali couldn't hold back as well and joined him. They burst into laughter, the nature of which was challenging to discern—happiness or sadness. Done with their meal, Chinmaya Babu remarked, "You're laughing. I am witnessing your laughter after so long."

"You, too, were laughing." Gitanjali laughed again, and Chinmaya Babu joined in, asking, "What was supposed to happen today has already happened. Will you cook something for the night, or should I eat the same puffed rice?"

Reconsidering, he said, "We don't usually cook at night. Why turn on the stove? Let's accept that this day is for us, and we must endure it." Uncertain, Gitanjali remained silent, perhaps contemplating whether to cook.

The sunset on the western horizon shrouded Gitanjali and Chinmaya Babu in the living room's darkness. With the night deepening, their silence grew.

Chinmaya Babu broke the silence, asking, "What have you been thinking?" Gitanjali replied, "What do you think of."

Chinmaya Babu sighed, saying, "What's the use of thinking anymore? I forgot to tell you, Gita, we haven't fulfilled our promise of feeding a hundred people for our son. I've repeatedly asked you to remind me, but today, I feel guilty." Chinmaya Babu cursed himself.

Trying to console him, Gitanjali said, "It's not your fault. You worked hard all your life for our son. How much time has passed? Feeding a hundred people is beyond our capacity. God knows that too..."

Chinmaya Babu stopped her, saying, "Let it be, Gita! Why talk about it today? Couldn't we even do this much for our son? It's one of the biggest failures of our lives."

Gitanjali replied, "Do you remember how many times we discussed the various prayers when our son was a child? We felt remorse for not being able to fulfil it."

Changing the topic, Chinmaya Babu said, "What does that boy say? When he grows up, he'll fulfil all his parents' wishes. Crazy kid."

Time passed, and they lost track of it. Emotions had seeped into their hearts unnoticed.

Another phone call surprised them. Frustrated, Chinmaya Babu declared, "We won't pick up the phone anymore. And if it's from the temple, I'll give them an earful."

Gitanjali pointed out, "How will you pick it up? The call has already ended."

"Let it be," Chinmaya Babu said. The phone rang again as he spoke, and he picked it up instantly. The voice on the other side stunned him.

"I heard the person from the temple caused you trouble by calling so many times. It wasn't my intention. I thought it would be wrong not to give your number as you decided to feed those people. I used a friend's help to feed the kids and did it myself. I would like to know if you two are relieved from the burden of keeping up that oath.

Chinmaya Babu, staring at Gitanjali, was delighted. He said, "Papuni has called. He was the one who placed the order at the temple and fed the kids. How happy those kids must have been!"

Chinmaya Babu held the phone to his ear again after hearing, "Hello.. hello". Then he heard, " Yes, I have been facing harm for a few days. Whatever business I'm taking over, I'm incurring loss. I wonder if it must have been due to the unfulfilled oath of the prayer you two had promised before the deity earlier. It compelled me to feed the kids. Otherwise, I had absolutely zero interest in this...."

The call ended, and Chinmaya Babu sprawled on the bed.

Gitanjali, horrified, said, "What happened? ..what did he say?"

Chinmaya Babu got disheartened to atone and dissolved into despair, "We couldn't fulfil the simple prayer for our son, and now he's in jeopardy."

Chinmaya Babu, silently blaming himself, said, "Shame on our life!"

Concerned, Gitanjali asked, "Why didn't you ask him to visit us?"

"Can a sculptor keep the sculpture he has crafted? Or a mason keeps the house he had built in his hands?"

Chinmaya Babu responded. "Our job was to sculpt, and we should be happy with it." Understanding, Gitanjali said, "If you can, please impale my chest."

After that, she indeed turned into a stone.

Black Eagle Books

www.blackeaglebooks.org
info@blackeaglebooks.org

Black Eagle Books, an independent publisher, was founded
as a nonprofit organization in April, 2019. It is our mission
to connect and engage the Indian diaspora and the world at
large with the best of works of world literature published
on a collaborative platform, with special emphasis on
foregrounding Contemporary Classics and New Writing.